SUMMER IN
BADEN-BADEN

Dostoyevsky's Last Home, St. Petersburg
Photographed by Leonid Tsypkin; used by courtesy of Mikhail Tsypkin

SUMMER IN BADEN-BADEN

A Novel

LEONID TSYPKIN

Translated from the Russian by Roger and Angela Keys
Introduction by Susan Sontag

A NEW DIRECTIONS BOOK

Manufactured in the United States of America
New Directions books are printed on acid-free paper.
Originally published in Russian as *Leto V Badene*. First published in English in
1987 by Quartet Books, Ltd. First published clothbound by New Directions in 2001.
Published simultaneously in Canada by Penguin Books Canada

Library of Congress Cataloging-in-Publication Data

Tsypkin, Leonid, d. 1982.
   [Leto v Badene. English]
   Summer in Baden-Baden / Leonid Tsypkin ;
   translated from the Russian by Roger and Angela Keys ; introduction by Susan
   Sontag.
   p. cm.
   Translation originally published: London: Quartet: 1987. With new introd.
   ISBN 0-8112-1484-2
   1. Dostoyevsky, Fyodor, 1821-1881—Fiction. I. Keys, Roger. II. Keys, Angela.
   II. Title.

   PG3489.S976 L4813 2001
   891.73'44—dc21   200132658

New Directions Books are published for James Laughlin
by New Directions Publishing Corporation,
80 Eighth Avenue, New York 10011

SECOND CLOTHBOUND PRINTING

DEDICATED TO KLARA MIKHAYLOVNA
ROZENTAL'

'And who knows . . . perhaps the only purpose which mankind aspires to in this world is the perpetual process of achievement, in other words – not any specific goal, but life itself.'

'How tiring, how arrogant are these tricks of yours, and yet at the same time how fearful you are!'
Fyodor Dostoyevsky
Notes from Underground

INTRODUCTION

The literature of the second half of the twentieth century is a much traversed field and it seems unlikely that there are still masterpieces in major, intently patrolled languages waiting to be discovered. Yet some ten years ago I came across just such a book, *Summer in Baden-Baden*, which I would include among the most beautiful, exalting, and original achievements of a century's worth of fiction and para-fiction.

The reasons for the book's obscurity are not hard to fathom. To begin with, its author was not by profession a writer. Leonid Tsypkin (1926–82) was a doctor—indeed, a distinguished medical researcher, who published more than a hundred papers in scientific journals in the Soviet Union and abroad. But—discard any comparisons with Chekhov and Bulgakov—this Russian doctor-writer never saw a single page of his literary work published during his lifetime.

Censorship and its intimidations are only part of the story. Tsypkin's fiction was, to be sure, a poor candidate for official publication. But it did not circulate in samizdat either, for Tsypkin remained—out of pride, intractable gloom, unwillingness to risk being rejected by the unofficial literary establishment—wholly outside the independent or underground literary circles that flourished in Moscow in the 1960s and 1970s, the era when he was writing "for the drawer." For literature itself.

Actually, it is something of a miracle that *Summer in Baden-Baden* survived at all.

To explain this miracle, and the world from which the novel emerged, it is necessary to tell something of its author's life.

(For what follows I am indebted to information generously supplied me by Leonid Tsypkin's son, Mikhail, and daughter-in-law, Elena, who emigrated to the United States in 1977 and live in California. A brief tribute by another émigré, Azary Messerer, entitled "Death of a Writer-Refusenik," which appeared in a Jewish magazine called *Et cetera* in 1983, the year after Tsypkin died, is, as far as I know, the only acknowledgment of Tsypkin's life in English.)

Leonid Tsypkin was born in 1926 in Minsk of Russian-Jewish parents, both physicians. The medical specialty of his mother, Vera Polyak, was pulmonary tuberculosis. His father, Boris Tsypkin, was an orthopedic surgeon, who, in 1934, was arrested on the usual fanciful charges and then released, through the intervention of an influential friend, after he tried to commit suicide by jumping down a prison stairwell. He returned home on a stretcher with a broken back, but he did not become an invalid and went on with his surgical practice until his death (at sixty-four) in 1961. Two of Boris Tsypkin's sisters and a brother perished during the Terror.

Minsk fell a week after the German invasion in 1941, and Boris Tsypkin's mother, another sister, and two little nephews were murdered in the Minsk ghetto. Boris Tsypkin and his wife and fifteen-year-old Leonid owed their escape from the city to the chairman of a nearby collective farm, a grateful ex-patient, who ordered several barrels of pickles taken off a truck to accommodate the esteemed orthopedic surgeon and his family.

A year later, Leonid Tsypkin began his medical studies, and when the war was over he returned with his parents to Minsk, where he graduated from medical school in 1947. In 1948, he married Natalya Michnikova, an economist. Mikhail, their only child, was born in 1950. By then, Stalin's anti-Semitic campaign, launched the year before, was racking up its victims, and Tsypkin managed to hide for the next years on the staff of a rural psychiatric hospital. In 1957, he was allowed to settle with his wife and son in Moscow, where he had been offered a post as a pathologist at the prestigious Institute for Poliomyelitis and Viral Encephalitis and became part of the team that introduced the Sabin polio vaccine in the Soviet Union; his subsequent work at the Institute reflected a variety of research interests, among them the response of tumor tissues to lethal viral infections and the biology and pathology of monkeys.

Tsypkin had always been passionate about literature, and always written a little for himself, both prose and poetry. In his early twenties, when he was nearing the completion of his medical studies, he had considered quitting medicine in order to study literature, with the idea of devoting himself entirely to writing. Riven by the nineteenth-century Russian soul questions (how to live without faith? without God?), he idolized Tolstoy. Eventually, Tolstoy was replaced by Dostoyevsky. Tsypkin also had cine-loves: Antonioni, for example, but not Tarkovsky. In the early 1960s, he thought about enrolling in night classes at the Institute of Cinematography to become a film director, but the necessity of supporting his family, he was to say, made him pull back.

It was also in the early 1960s that Tsypkin began a more committed spate of writing: poems which, according to his son, were strongly influenced by Tsvetaeva and Pasternak, whose pictures hung above his small work table. In September 1965, Tsypkin decided to chance showing some of his lyrics to Andrei Sinyavsky, but Sinyavsky was arrested a few days before their appointment. Tsypkin and Sinyavsky, who was a year older, were never to meet, and Tsypkin became even more cautious. ("My father," says Mikhail Tsypkin, "was not inclined to talk or even to think much about politics. In our family, it was assumed without discussion that the Soviet regime was Evil incarnate.") After several unsuccessful attempts to publish some of these poems, Tsypkin stopped writing for a while. Much of his time was devoted to finishing "A Study of the Morphological and Biological Properties of Cell Cultures of Trypsinized Tissues," his dissertation for the advanced doctorate (the Doctor of Science degree). (His earlier dissertation, for the Ph.D., was a study of growth rates of brain tumors that had been subjected to repeated surgeries.) Once the second dissertation was defended, in 1969, Tsypkin received an increase in salary, which freed him from moonlighting as a part-time pathologist in a small hospital. Already in his forties, he began writing again—not poetry but prose.

In the eleven years he had left to live, Tsypkin created a small body of prose of ever larger reach and complexity. After a handful of short sketches came longer, more plotted stories, then two autobiographical novellas, *The Bridge Across the Neroch* and *Norartakir*, and then the novel, *Summer in Baden-Baden*, his last book. According to his son,

> Every day, he left at a quarter to eight sharp for his work at the Institute of Poliomyelitis and Viral Encephalitis, situated in a distant suburb of Moscow, not far from the Vnukovo airport. He came back home at six p.m., had dinner, took a short nap, and sat down to write—if not his prose, then his medical research papers. Before going to bed, at ten p.m., he sometimes would take a walk. He usually spent his weekends writing as well; for a change, he would work at the Lenin Library, gathering materials for his book on Dostoyevsky.
>
> My father craved every opportunity to write, but writing was difficult, painful. He agonized over each word, and endlessly corrected his hand-written manuscripts. Once finished with editing, he typed his prose on an ancient, shiny German typewriter, "Erika"—World War II loot, sold by one owner to the next until an uncle gave it to my father in 1949. And in that form his writings remained. He did not send his manuscripts to publishers, and did not want to circulate his prose in samizdat because he was afraid of problems with the KGB and of losing his job.

Writing without hope or prospect of being published—what resources of faith in literature does that imply? Tsypkin's readership was not much larger than his wife, his son, and a couple of his son's Moscow University classmates. He had no real friends in any of the Moscow literary worlds.

True, there was one literary person in his immediate family. This was Tsypkin's mother's younger sister, the literary critic Lydia Polyak, and readers of *Summer in Baden-Baden* make her glancing acquaintance on the very first page. Aboard a train bound for Leningrad, the narrator—Tsypkin—opens a book, a precious book whose binding and decorative bookmark are lovingly described before we learn that it is the *Reminiscences* of Dostoyevsky's second wife, Anna Grigoryevna Dostoyevsky, and that this copy, flimsy and almost falling apart when it came into Tsypkin's hands, belongs to an unnamed aunt who can only be Lydia Polyak. Since, Tsypkin writes, "in my heart of hearts I had no intention of returning the book borrowed from my aunt who possessed a large library," he has had it trimmed and rebound.

According to Mikhail Tsypkin, several of his father's stories contain a cranky reference to Polyak. A well-connected member of the Moscow intelligentsia for half a century, she had held a research position at the Gorky Institute of World Literature since the 1930s, and even when she was fired from her teaching post at Moscow University during the anti-Semitic purges of the early 1950s, she managed to keep her position at the Gorky Institute, where Sinyavsky eventually became a junior colleague of hers. Although it was she who arranged the aborted meeting with Sinyavsky, Polyak disapproved of her nephew's writing and condescended to him, for which he never forgave her.

In 1977, Tsypkin's son and daughter-in-law decided to apply for exit visas. Before they applied, Natalya Michnikova resigned from her job in the division of the State Committee of Supplies (GOSSNAB) that allocated heavy road-building and construction equipment to all sectors of the Soviet economy, including the military, in the hope that this employment, for which a security clearance was needed, would not prejudice her son's chances. The visas were granted, and Mikhail and Elena Tsypkin left for the United States. As soon as the KGB relayed this information to the director of the Institute for Poliomyelitis and Viral Encephalitis, Sergei Drozdov, retaliation was inevitable. Tsypkin was demoted to junior researcher—the position of someone without an advanced degree (he had two) and his starting rank of more than twenty years earlier—and his salary (now the couple's only source of income) cut by seventy-five percent. He continued to go to the Institute every day but was excluded from laboratory research, which was always conducted by teams: not one of his colleagues was willing to work with Tsypkin for fear of being tainted by contact with an "undesirable element." And there was no point in seeking a research position elsewhere, since in every job application he would have to declare that his son had emigrated.

In June 1979, Tsypkin, his wife, and his mother applied for

exit visas. They then waited almost two years. In April 1981, they were called into the Moscow visa office and told that their requests were "inexpedient" and had been turned down. (Emigration from the USSR virtually stopped in 1980, when relations with the United States deteriorated as a result of the Soviet invasion of Afghanistan; it became obvious that, for the time being, no favors from Washington would be forthcoming in exchange for permitting Soviet Jews to leave.) It was in this period that Tsypkin wrote most of *Summer in Baden-Baden*.

He had started the book in 1977 and he completed it in 1980. The writing was preceded by years of consulting archives and of photographing places associated with Dostoyevsky's life as well as ones frequented by Dostoyevsky's characters during the seasons and at the times of day mentioned in the novels. (Tsypkin was a dedicated amateur photographer, and had owned a camera since the early 1950s.) After finishing *Summer in Baden-Baden*, he presented an album of these photographs to the Dostoyevsky Museum in Leningrad.

However inconceivable it was that *Summer in Baden-Baden* could be published in Russia, there was still the option of publishing it abroad, as the best writers were now doing with their work. Tsypkin finally decided to attempt just this, and asked a journalist friend who had received permission to leave in early 1981, Azary Messerer, to smuggle a copy of the manuscript and some of the photographs out of the Soviet Union, which Messerer was able to do with the help of two American friends, a married couple, who were Moscow-based correspondents for UPI.

At the end of September 1981, Tsypkin, his wife, and his mother reapplied for exit visas. On October 15th, Vera Polyak died at the age of eighty-six. The refusal of the visa applications for all three came a week later: this time, the decision had taken less than a month.

In early March 1982, Tsypkin went to see the head of the Moscow visa office, who told him: "Doctor, you will never be allowed to emigrate." On Monday, March 15th, Sergei Drozdov informed Tsypkin that he would no longer be kept on at the Institute. The same day, Tsypkin's son, who was in graduate school at Harvard, called Moscow to announce that on Saturday his father had finally become a published writer. Azary Messerer had succeeded in placing *Summer in Baden-Baden* with a Russian-émigré weekly in New York, *Novaya Gazeta,* which would be serializing the novel. The first installment, illustrated by some of Tsypkin's photographs, had appeared on March 13th.

On Saturday, March 20th, which was Tsypkin's fifty-sixth birthday, Natalya Michnikova telephoned her son. That morning in Moscow, Leonid Tsypkin had been working at his desk on the translation of a medical text from English into Russian—translating being one of the few ways of eking out a living open to *refuseniks* (Soviet citizens, usually Jews, who had been denied exit visas and fired from their jobs)—when he suddenly felt unwell (it was a heart attack), lay down, called out to his wife, and died. He had been a published author of fiction for exactly seven days.

For Tsypkin, it was a matter of honor that everything of a factual nature in *Summer in Baden-Baden* be true to the story and the circumstances of the real lives it evokes. This is not, like J.M. Coetzee's wonderful *The Master of Petersburg*, a Dostoyevsky fantasy. Neither is it a docu-novel, although Tsypkin was obsessed with getting everything "right." (In his son's words, he was, in all matters, "very systematic.") It is possible that Tsypkin imagined that if *Summer in Baden-Baden* were ever published as a book it should include some of the photographs he had taken, thereby anticipating the signature effect of the work of W.G. Sebald, who, by seeding his books with photographs, infuses the plainest idea of verisimilitude with enigma and pathos.

What kind of a book is *Summer in Baden-Baden*? From the start, it proposes a double narrative. It is wintertime, late December, no date given: a species of "now." A narrator is on a train going to Leningrad (once and future St. Petersburg). And it is mid-April 1867. The newly married Dostoyevskys, Fyodor ("Fedya"), and his young wife, Anna Grigoryevna, have left St. Petersburg and are on their way to Dresden. The account of the Dostoyevskys' travels—for they will be mostly abroad in Tsypkin's novel, and not only in Baden-Baden—has been scrupulously researched. The passages where the narrator—Tsypkin—describes his own doings are autobiographical. Since imagination and fact are easily contrasted, we tend to draw genre lessons from this, and segregate invented stories (fiction) from real-life narratives (chronicle and autobiography). That's one convention—ours. In Japanese literature, the so-called "I-novel" (*shishōsetsu*), a narrative that is essentially autobiographical but contains elements of invention, is one of the dominant novel forms.

In *Summer in Baden-Baden*, several "real" worlds are being evoked, described, recreated in a hallucinatory rush of feeling. The originality of Tsypkin's novel lies in the way it *moves*, from the displacements of the never-to-be-named narrator, embarked on his journey through the bleak contemporary Soviet landscape, to the trials of the peripatetic Dostoyevskys. In the cultural ruin that is the present, the feverish past shines through. Tsypkin is traveling *into* Fedya's and Anna's souls and bodies, as he travels *to* Leningrad. There are prodigious, uncanny acts of empathy.

Tsypkin will stay in Leningrad for a few days: it is a Dostoyevsky pilgrimage (surely not the first), a solitary one (no doubt as usual), that will end in a visit to the Dostoyevsky Museum. The Dostoyevskys are just beginning their impecunious travels; they will remain in Western Europe for four years. (It is worth recalling that the author of *Summer in Baden-Baden* was never allowed outside the Soviet Union.) Dresden, Baden-Baden, Basel, Frankfurt, Paris—their lot is to be constantly agitated, by the confusions and humiliations of cramping financial misery while having to negotiate with a chorus of presumptuous foreigners (porters, coachmen, landladies, waiters, shopkeepers, pawnbrokers, croupiers) and by gusts of whim and volatile emotions of many kinds. The gambling fever. The moral fevers. The fever of illness. The sensual fevers. The fever of jealousy. The penitential fevers. The fear . . .

The principal intensity depicted in Tsypkin's fictional recreation of Dostoyevsky's life is not gambling, not writing, not Christing. It is the searing, generous absoluteness (which is not to pronounce on the satisfactoriness) of conjugal love. Who can forget the image of the couple's lovemaking as swimming?

Anna's all-forgiving but always dignified love for Fedya rhymes with the love of literature's disciple, Tsypkin, for Dostoyevsky.

Nothing is invented. Everything is invented. The framing action of this short book is the trip the narrator is making to the sites of Dostoyevsky's life and novels, part of the preparation (as we come to realize) for the book we hold in our hands. *Summer in Baden-Baden* belongs to a rare and exquisitely ambitious subgenre of the novel: a retelling of the life of a real person of accomplishment from another era, it interweaves this story with a story in the present, of the novelist mulling over, trying to gain deeper entry into, the inner life of someone whose destiny it was to have become not only historical but monumental. (Another example, and one of the glories of twentieth-century Italian literature, is *Artemisia* by Anna Banti.)

Tsypkin leaves Moscow on the first page and two-thirds of the way through the book arrives at the Moscow Station in Leningrad. Although aware that somewhere near the station is the "ordinary, grey Petersburg dwelling-house" where Dostoyevsky spent the last years of his life, he walks onward with his suitcase in the icy nocturnal gloom, crossing the Nevsky Prospect to pass other places associated with Dostoyevsky's last years, then turns up where he always stays when in Leningrad, a portion of a dilapidated communal apartment occupied by a tenderly described intimate of his mother, who welcomes him, feeds him, makes up a broken sofa for him to sleep on, and asks him, as she always does, "Are you still as keen on Dostoyevsky?" When she goes to bed, Tsypkin sinks into a volume plucked at random from her bookcase's pre-Revolutionary edition of Dostoyevsky's collected works, his *Diary of a Writer*, and falls asleep musing about the mystery of Dostoyevsky's anti-Semitism.

After a morning spent chatting with his affectionate old friend, and hearing more of her stories of the horrors endured during the Leningrad Blockade, Tsypkin sets off—the short winter day is already darkening—to roam about the city, "taking photographs of the Raskolnikov House or the Old Money-lender's House or Sonechka's House or buildings where their author had lived during the darkest and most clandestine period of his life in the years immediately following his return from exile." Walking on, "led by a kind of instinct," Tsypkin manages to reach "exactly the right spot"—"my heart was pounding with joy and some other vaguely sensed feeling"— opposite the four-story corner building where Dostoyevsky died, which is now the Dostoyevsky Museum; and the description of the visit ("an almost churchlike silence reigned in the museum") segues into a narrative of a dying that is worthy of Tolstoy. It is through the prism of Anna's excruciating grief that Tsypkin recreates the long deathbed hours in this book about love, conjugal love and the love of literature—loves that are in no way linked or compared, but each given its due, each contributing its infusing fire.

Loving Dostoyevsky, what is one to do—what is a Jew to do— with the knowledge that he hated Jews? How explain the vicious anti-Semitism of "a man so sensitive in his novels to the suffering of others, this jealous defender of the insulted and injured"? And how understand "this special attraction which Dostoyevsky seems to possess for Jews"?

The most intellectually powerful of the earlier Jewish Dostoyevsky lovers is Leonid Grossman (1888-1965), who heads a long list of Jewish Dostoyevskyists cited by Tsypkin. Grossman is an important source for Tsypkin's re-imagining of Dostoyevsky's life, and the book the narrator is reading at the beginning of *Summer in Baden-Baden* is the product of Grossman's scholarly labors. It was he who edited the first selection of Anna Dostoyevsky's *Reminiscences*, which were published in 1925, seven years after her death. Tsypkin speculates that the absence of "loathsome little Jews" and other such phrases in the memoirs of Dostoyevsky's widow may be explained by the fact that she wrote them, on the eve of the Revolution, after she had made Grossman's acquaintance.

Tsypkin must have been familiar with Grossman's many influential essays on Dostoyevsky, such as *Balzac and Dostoyevsky* (1914) and *Dostoyevsky's Library* (1919). He may have come across Grossman's Dostoyevsky novel, *Roulettenburg* (1932), a gloss on Dostoyevsky's own novella about the gambling passion. (*Roulettenburg* was the original title of *The*

Gambler.) But he couldn't have read Grossman's *Confessions of a Jew* (1924), which had gone completely out of circulation. *Confessions of a Jew* is an account of the life of the most enthralling and pathetic of the Jewish Dostoyevskyists, Arkady Kovner (1842–1909), a reckless autodidact who had been brought up in the Vilna ghetto, with whom Dostoyevsky entered into an epistolary relationship. Kovner had fallen under the writer's spell and was inspired by reading *Crime and Punishment* to commit a theft to succor an ailing impoverished young woman with whom he was in love. In 1875, from his cell in a Moscow jail, before being transported to serve a sentence of four years of hard labor in Siberia, Kovner wrote to Dostoyevsky to challenge him on the matter of his antipathy to Jews. (That was the first letter; the second was about the immortality of the soul.)

In the end, there is no resolution of the anguishing subject of Dostoyevsky's anti-Semitism, a theme that comes surging into *Summer in Baden-Baden* once Tsypkin reaches Leningrad. It seemed, he writes,

> strange to the point of implausibility . . . that this man should not have come up with even a single word in the defense or justification of a people persecuted over several thousand years . . . and he did not even refer to the Jews as a people, but as a tribe . . . and to this tribe I belonged and the many friends and acquaintances of mine with whom I had discussed the subtlest problems of Russian literature.

Yet this hasn't kept Jews from loving Dostoyevsky. Tsypkin has no better explanation than the fervor of Jews for the greatness of Russian literature—which may remind us that the German adulation of Goethe and Schiller was in large part a Jewish affair, right up to the time Germany started killing its Jews. Loving Dostoyevsky means loving literature.

A crash course on all the great themes of Russian literature, *Summer in Baden-Baden* is unified by the ingenuity and velocity of its language (according to Tsypkin's son, superbly rendered in English by Roger and Angela Keys), which moves boldly, seductively, between first and third person—the doings, memories, reflections of the narrator ("I") and the Dostoyevsky scenes ("he," "they," "she")—and between past and present. But this is not a unitary present (of the narrator, Tsypkin, on his Dostoyevsky pilgrimage), any more than it is a unitary past (the Dostoyevskys from 1867 to 1881, the year of Dostoyevsky's death). Dostoyevsky, in the past, submits to the undertow of remembered scenes, passions from earlier moments of his life; the narrator, in the present, summons up memories of *his* past.

Each paragraph indent begins a long, long sentence, whose connectives are "and" (many of these) and "but" (several) and "although" and "and so" and "whereas" and "just as" and "because" and "as if," along with many dashes, and there is a full stop only when the paragraph ends. In the course of these ardently protracted paragraph-sentences, the river of feeling gathers up and sweeps along the narrative of Dostoyevsky's life and Tsypkin's: a sentence that starts with Fedya and Anna in Dresden might then flash back to Dostoyevsky's convict years or to an earlier bout of gambling mania linked to his romance with Polina Suslova, then thread onto this a memory from the narrator's medical-student days and a rumination on some lines by Pushkin.

Tsypkin's sentences call to mind José Saramago's run-on sentences, which fold dialogue into description and description into dialogue, spiked by verbs that refuse to stay consistently either in the past or the present tense. In their *incessantness*, Tsypkin's sentences have something of the same force and hectic authority as those of Thomas Bernhard. Obviously, Tsypkin could not have known the books of Saramago and Bernhard. He had other models of ecstatic prose in twentieth-century literature. He loved the early (not the late) prose of Pasternak—*Safe Conduct*, not *Doctor Zhivago*. He loved Tsvetaeva. He loved Rilke, in part because Tsvetaeva and Pasternak had loved Rilke; he read very little foreign literature, and only in translation. Of what he had read, his greatest passion was Kafka, whom he discovered by way of a volume of stories published in the Soviet Union in the early 1960s. The amazing Tsypkin sentence was entirely his own invention.

Reminiscing about his father, Tsypkin's son describes him

as obsessed by detail and compulsively neat. His daughter-in-law, commenting on his choice of medical specialty—pathology—and his decision never to practice as a clinical physician, recalls that "he was very interested in death." Perhaps only an obsessive, death-haunted hypochondriac, such as Tsypkin seems to have been, could have devised a sentence-form that is free in so original a way. His prose is an ideal vehicle for the emotional intensity and abundance of his subject. In a relatively short book, the long sentence bespeaks inclusiveness and associativeness, the passionate agility of a temperament steeped, in most respects, in adamancy.

Besides the account of the incomparable Dostoyevsky, what can one *not* find in this extraordinary mental adventure that is Tsypkin's novel? Taken for granted, if that is not too odd a way of putting it, are the sufferings of the Soviet era, from the Great Terror of 1934–37 to the present of the narrator's quest: the book pulses with them. *Summer in Baden-Baden* is also a spirited and plangent account of Russian literature—the whole arc of Russian literature. Pushkin, Turgenev (there is a scene of fierce confrontation between Dostoyevsky and Turgenev), and the great figures of twentieth-century Russian literature and ethical struggle—Tsvetaeva, Solzhenitsyn, Sakharov and Bonner—also enter, are poured into the narration.

If you want from one book an experience of the depth and authority of Russian literature, read this book. If you want a novel that can fortify your soul and give you a larger idea of feeling, and of breathing, read this book.

Susan Sontag
July 2001

SUMMER IN BADEN-BADEN

I was on a train, travelling by day, but it was winter-time –
late December, the very depths – and to add to it the train
was heading north – to Leningrad – so it was quickly
darkening on the other side of the windows – bright lights of
Moscow stations flashing into view and vanishing again
behind me like the scattering of some invisible hand – each
snow-veiled suburban platform with its fleeting row of
lamps melting into one fiery ribbon – the dull drone of a
station rushing past, as if the train were roaring over a bridge
– the sound muffled by the double-glazed windows with
frames not quite hermetically sealed into fogged-up, half-
frozen panes of glass – pierced even so by the station-lights
forcefully etching their line of fire – and beyond, the sense of
boundless snowy wastes – and the violent sway of the
carriage from side to side – pitching and rolling – especially
in the end corridor – and outside, once complete darkness
had fallen and only the hazy whiteness of snow was visible
and the surburban dachas had come to an end and in the
window along with me was the reflection of the carriage with
its ceiling-lights and seated passengers, I took from the
suitcase in the rack above me a book I had already started to
read in Moscow and which I had brought especially for the
journey to Leningrad, and I opened it at the page held by a
bookmark decorated with Chinese characters and a delicate
oriental drawing – and in my heart of hearts I had no
intention of returning the book borrowed from my aunt who
possessed a large library, and because it was very flimsy and
almost falling apart, I had taken it to a binder who trimmed
the pages so that they lay together evenly and enclosed the

whole thing in a strong cover on which he pasted the book's original title-page – the *Diary* of Anna Grigor'yevna Dostoyevskaya produced by some liberal publishing-house still possible at that time – either 'Landmarks', or 'New Life', or one of those – with dates given in both Old Style and New Style and words and whole phrases in German or French without translation and the *de rigueur* 'Mme' added with all the diligence of a grammar-school pupil – a transliteration of the shorthand notes which she had taken during the summer following her marriage abroad.

The Dostoyevskys had left Petersburg in mid-April 1867, arriving in Vilna by the following morning where they were constantly pestered by loathsome little Jews thrusting their services upon them on the hotel stairs and even going as far as chasing after the horse-cab in which Anna Grigor'yevna and Fyodor Mikhaylovich were travelling, trying, until they were sent packing, to sell them amber cigarette-holders – and the same Jews with flowing uncut curls framing their brows could be seen in the evening walking their Jewish wives around the narrow old streets – and then a day or two later, off to Berlin and then to Dresden where they began to look round for an apartment, because Germans, and especially German women – all these Fräulein-proprietors of boarding-houses and even of simple furnished rooms – ruthlessly overcharged and underfed newly arrived Russians – waiters cheated them out of their small change, and not just waiters either – the German race was a dim-witted bunch as it seemed collectively incapable of explaining to Fedya how to get to any street whatsoever, invariably pointing in the wrong direction – it seemed almost deliberate – and Anna Grigor'yevna was an old hand at Jew-spotting from when she had first visited Fedya while he was writing *Crime and Punishment* at the Olonkin house, which, as Anna Grigor'yevna was to observe later, immediately reminded her of the house in which Raskol'nikov lived – and Jews could be nosed out there, too, scurrying up and down the stairs among the other tenants – but, to be quite fair, it should be stated that in the *Memoirs* which Anna Grigor'-yevna wrote not long before the Revolution, perhaps even after she got to know Leonid Grossman, there is no mention at all of loathsome little Jews on stairs.

The photograph pasted into the *Diary* shows Anna Grigor'yevna still quite young at the time, her glowering face both possessed and pious, but Fedya, already getting on in years, not very tall and with such short legs that it seemed, if he were to get up from the chair on which he was sitting, he would not appear very much taller – he had the face of a man of the common people, and it was obvious that he liked to have his photograph taken and that he was a fervent man of prayer – so why had I rushed around Moscow shaking with emotion (I am not ashamed to admit it) with the *Diary* in my hands until I found someone to bind it? – Why, in public on a tram, had I avidly leafed through its flimsy pages, looking for places which I seemed to have glimpsed before, and then why, after seeing it bound, had I carefully placed the book, which had now become heavy, on my desk like the Bible, keeping it there day and night? – Why was I now on my way to Petersburg – yes, not to Leningrad, but precisely to *Petersburg* whose streets had been walked by this short-legged, rather small individual (no more so, probably, than most other inhabitants of the nineteenth century) with the face of a church-warden or a retired soldier? – Why was I reading this book *now*, in a railway-carriage, beneath a wavering, flickering, electric light-bulb, glaring brightly at one moment, almost extinguished the next according to the speed of the train and the performance of the diesel locomotives, amid the slamming of doors at either end of the carriage by people constantly coming through balancing glasses full of water for children or for washing fruit, leaving for a smoke, or simply to go to the toilet, whose door would bang shut immediately afterwards? – amid the banging and slamming of all these doors, with the rolling motion jogging my book now to one side, now to the other, and the smell of coal and steam engines which somehow still lingered although they had stopped running long ago.

They eventually rented a room from Mme Zimmermann, a tall, angular Swiss, but on the very day of their arrival they booked in at a hotel on the main square and immediately made their way to the picture-gallery.

3

An enormous queue converging on the Pushkin Museum in Moscow – small groups only being admitted at a time – the 'Sistine Madonna' hanging on a landing somewhere between floors, a militiaman in situ beneath – and years later at the same museum the 'Mona Lisa' displayed herself, strategically lit, behind double, bullet-proof panes of glass – the queue of 'connected' people snaking its way towards the painting or, rather, to the glass armour-plating – an embalmed corpse in a sarcophagus, Madonna in a landscape background – a truly enigmatic smile or, perhaps, just the effect of public opinion – and beside the picture, another militiaman, urging the queue forward with a 'Take your leave *now*, take your leave!' in decorous fashion, as they all, of course, were art experts or special guests – trying to linger as long as they could beside the painting and, when they had passed it by, catching up with the people who had gone on ahead, continuing to peer back at the picture, cricking their necks, revolving their heads nearly a hundred and eighty degrees – the 'Sistine Madonna', however, hung on a wall between two windows, the light falling from the side – the day was cloudy and the painting seemed veiled with a kind of haze – the Madonna floated in clouds which seemed like the airborne hem of her dress or perhaps the two things melted together – and somewhere down below to the left an apostle looked piously up – with six fingers on one hand – really six, I counted them myself – and a photograph of this picture was given to Dostoyevsky for his birthday many years after his visit to Dresden and shortly before his death, by someone supposing that this was his favourite picture (although it was probably 'Christ in the Sepulchre' by Holbein the Younger) – and anyway the photograph of Raphael's 'Sistine Madonna', in a wooden frame, hangs in the Dostoyevsky Museum in Leningrad above the leather couch on which the writer died – an airborne Madonna holding an equally airborne half-seated child in her arms, perhaps offering him her breast like a gypsy woman, in front of anyone – her expression as enigmatic as the Mona Lisa's – a photograph just like that, a little smaller and probably not as good as a modern print, can be found on a shelf in my aunt's glass-fronted book-case, positioned with a somewhat deliberate carelessness.

The Dostoyevskys would visit the art-gallery every day in the same way as people in Kislovodsk drop into the kursaal to take the waters, for a rendezvous or simply to stand about observing the comings and goings, and then go to lunch – looking for a cheaper-style restaurant, but a place which would provide them with good food and trustworthy waiters – always the Dostoyevskys found they were cheated out of two or three silver groschen as all Germans were undeniably unscrupulous – after the usual gallery visit they once chose the Brühlsche Terrasse, placed picturesquely over the Elbe – the waiter had been spotted on a previous visit and dubbed the 'diplomat', as he looked like one – and into the bargain they had caught him charging twice the price for a cup of coffee – five groschen instead of two and a half – but they outsmarted him when Anna Grigor'yevna had slipped him the two and a half groschen, given them as change, back to him as a tip in place of five – but this time they were very hungry, especially Fedya, and instead of attending their table, the 'diplomat' busied himself with a later arrival, some Saxon officer with fleshy red nose and yellowish eyes, his whole appearance that of a drinker – and although Fedya called to the waiter, he continued, with imperturbable expression, to serve the officer who was adjusting the starched napkin behind his tight military collar – revenge by the 'diplomat' for their last encounter – Fedya tapped his knife on the table – and finally the 'diplomat' arrived, but only, of course, in passing, to say that he could in fact hear them and there was no need to drum on the table – chicken again for Fedya and veal cutlets – much later one portion only of chicken arriving – 'What is the meaning of this,' – and the 'diplomat' replied with excessive politeness that only one portion was ordered – and the same thing again with the veal cutlets – and four waiters sat playing cards in the next dining-room, and in the room where the Dostoyevskys ate there were few customers – he must have done it on purpose – red blotches sprouted on Fedya's face, and loudly to his wife he said that, if he had been there alone, he would have shown them, and he even began to shout at her as if it were her fault that the two of them had gone there together – and with knife and fork poised he purposely hurled them down with a great crash, nearly smashing the plate – people began to stare – and they left without looking around, Fedya having thrown a whole thaler onto the table instead of the twenty-three groschen they owed – and, slamming the door so hard that the panes of glass shook, they set off down the chestnut-lined avenue – he walking resolutely ahead, she behind, scarcely able to keep up – without her, he could have seen the business through and insisted on his own way, but in fact he was now walking away humiliated by that villainous waiter, because all waiters were, of course, villains – the embodiment of the basest features of human nature – but, alas! the remnants of this cursed waiter-strain linger in all of us – had he himself not stared sycophantically into the yellow-lynx eyes of that drunk, red-nosed swine of a commandant in the convict prison? – yes! that was the one brought to mind by the Saxon officer just now – the one who, drunk and chaperoned by guards, had burst into their wooden barrack and, spotting a prisoner in grey-black jacket backed with its yellow ace of diamonds, spotting him lying down there on the bunk because he felt unwell that particular day, unable to work, had bellowed with all the strength of his bullish throat: 'Up, you! Over here!' – and he had been that prisoner, the man now walking down a chestnut-lined avenue away from that restaurant and that terrace, so picturesquely placed over the Elbe – and even then, in the convict-prison, he had seen it all only from the side, as if it happened in a dream, or to someone else, not to him at all – and being present in the guard-house once, when corporal punishment was being applied – the victim lying motionless as he was beaten with birch-rods, leaving bloody weals on his back and buttocks – just as silently the prisoner slowly rose to his feet, carefully fastened each button on his jacket and left the room, without so much as a glance at Krivtsov who stood there beside him – would *he* have managed to keep so silent and leave the guard-room with such dignity? – jumping up off his bunk and feverishly shaking hands adjusting the grey-black jacket, he walked towards Krivtsov who stood in the doorway – walked with head lowered – no, not walked, but almost ran – humiliating in itself – and when he reached the officer, he stared at him, not a firm, hard look, but with pleading eyes – realizing this from the way Krivtsov's pupils dilated like a predator's, the pupils of those yellow, lynx-eyes of his – lynx-like not only through their animal shape, but because of that hunting look, searching for the next victim – the thought running through his mind even as he stood before him, and that he could think of such a thing at such a moment had struck him at the time as strange – and what was this to do with servility?! – this fear, this simple fear – but fear gives rise to servility, does it not?

Anna Grigor'yevna managed to catch him up and, placing her hand with its worn glove beneath his elbow, looked guiltily into his eyes – without her, *he* would have shown that waiter what's what, *he* would have put them all in their place! – his eyes moving slowly away from her face, staring at the hand which lay on his shoulder – 'It does not befit a neatly dressed woman to be seen in such gloves,' he said slowly, distinctly, transferring his gaze to her face once again – with lips trembling and eye-lids strangely swelling up, she continued to walk by his side, but only through inertia and because she thought that his words could not apply to her: he would not have said that to *her* – with quickening pace she left him, almost at a run, turning into some side-street, also lined with chestnut trees – she looked round briefly and, through the leaves and her tears, could make out his figure marching down the avenue, resolute as ever, wearing the dark-grey almost black suit, bought in Berlin – at the time the thought had not occurred to him to suggest that she might buy herself some new gloves, although the ones she had already had frayed at the seams, and twice on the journey she had had to sew them up – in his presence – and now *he* reproached *her* for *that*, *and* the money for their journey had been obtained by pawning her mother's things – walking down the street, almost running, she kept close to the walls of the buildings, veil raised so that no-one could see her tear-swollen face – coming towards her, the occasional respectable bowler-hatted German out for a walk with his German wife, and their faces looked pink and self-satisfied – holding the hands of their children, clean and neatly dressed – and *they* didn't worry over paying for the day's lunch or dinner, and *they* didn't raise their voices at each other – and yet Fedya had shouted at her in the restaurant – slipping in through the door of their house she tried to avoid being seen – and first she entered the big room they used as a dining-room, oleographs on the wall depicting some river – the Rhine, probably – trees reflected in it, or castles perched on mountains against backgrounds of false blue skies – then the second room, their bedroom with two cumbersome beds, and then the third, a tiny room, Fedya's, with a desk and, lying on it, a neat white paper pile and some *papirosa* cigarettes with tobacco spilling out – and she suddenly realized she had come in here in the secret hope that he had overtaken her and would be waiting for her – then she left for the post-office where Fedya often called in, and he was not there and there were no letters, and she went back home again – surely he must be home by now? – Mme Zimmermann on the stairs told her that Fedya had come in and gone out somewhere – outside again, running on to the street, and suddenly she saw him – coming towards her, pale and smiling guiltily, even pleadingly – and so it turned out he had gone back to the terrace, thinking she would have returned there, demonstrating her independence, and then he had gone to look in the reading-room – and so they went indoors for a moment to change clothes because it was coming on to rain – pouring down in bucketfuls as they emerged again, but they did, after all, have to have lunch – three courses at the Hotel Victoria cost them two thalers and ten silber-groschen – a terrible price seeing that each cutlet cost twelve silbergroschen – have you ever seen the like! – a thoroughly unlucky day! – it was eight o'clock at night when they left the restaurant, dark and wet – so she opened her umbrella, but not in the prudent German way – it brushed against a passing German – and Fedya shouted because her clumsiness could be misinterpreted – and her eyes began to swell again, and in the darkness nobody noticed, thank God! – home again, side by side, not talking, as if they were strangers, and at home they tried to quarrel over tea, though it had all been said already, and then she mentioned his projected trip to Bad Homburg, and he started shouting again, and in reply she shouted back and went into the bedroom – he locked himself in his study, but later came to kiss her goodnight – a nightly habit, especially after a quarrel or disagreement – the gentle awakening to caress or kiss her, because she was his and within his power was her happiness or misery – his awareness of total power over this ingénue, playing with her at will, was probably like the feeling which I have towards sleek young dogs who, at the sight of a hand stretched out for a stroke, wag their tails in a nervous, pleading way, flatten themselves against the ground and begin to tremble – it began with the kiss, then his lips on her breasts, then the swimming began – swimming with large strokes, thrusting their arms in unison from the water to take great gulps of air into their lungs, further and further from the shore, towards the deep-blue arch of the sea – but inevitably he found he was swept into counter-currents bearing him away at an angle, almost back on himself, and he could not keep up, as her arms continued to thrust from the water, still in rhythm, to vanish into the distance – and he felt that he no longer swam but floundered about in the water, his feet reaching for the bottom – and strangely this current, bearing him away, preventing him from moving with her, seemed to turn into the yellow eyes of the commandant with dilated predator pupils and into the rushed unbuttoning of his convict's jacket in order to prostrate himself over the low oak table in the centre of the guard-house polished by thousands of bodies, and into the groans he could not suppress when the blows of the birch rods rained down, as if someone tightened a red-hot wire across his muscles and bones, and into the spasms of pain which began after the beating, and into the mocking or pitying faces of the onlookers, and into the satisfied smile of the commandant as he ordered the doctor to be summoned, turning sharply on his heels to march out of the guard-room – and the same thing happened with other women because, like Anya, they had all been invisible witnesses, peering through the metal grilled windows, or through the guard-house door, as they struggled to enter to plead on his behalf, but they were barred – all witnesses of his humiliation, and he hated them for that because it denied him experience of the full flight of his feelings – and today as well was added the insulting impudent look of that waiter and the face of the Saxon officer, so like that of the commandant.

A while back he had noticed a particular chair in the gallery where the 'Sistine Madonna' hung, a soft chair with a curved back which seemed to be set apart from the others which were placed there for visitors to rest or to sit on and admire one of the pictures – and nobody seemed to sit on this one chair – perhaps meant for the attendant or possessing some historical value – and the first time the thought became tangible, a shiver ran down his spine, it seemed so audacious, so inconceivable – preparing himself for action, he passed the chair and once almost placed his foot on it, but a lot of people were in the room, and the bored-looking attendant dressed in his uniform jacket was leaning against the wall – and perhaps he should have done exactly that in front of everyone, the attendant in particular, as preventing this kind of thing was precisely an attendant's job – approaching the chair, his heart would stop, and after a second of hesitation, as if pondering which way to walk round the chair, he would pass by, peering at the Madonna with exaggerated interest – but that night, as Anya swam away so distantly and he floundered somewhere near the shore, unable to reach the bottom – that night he made a solemn vow to do exactly that – and so, entering the gallery as usual next morning, he headed immediately for the room where the 'Sistine Madonna' hung, the beat of his heart echoing in his ears, a crowd jostling in front of the painting – some standing or sitting a slight distance away with opera-glasses (easier to look with *them* as your eyes were concentrated on the painting and did not wander) – and at first not seeing the chair and, from the way his heart stopped jumping and fluttering, realizing he was inwardly glad – but the chair was simply hidden by people – and there was the attendant, in full livery with gilded buttons – a purposeful walk towards the chair, even pushing his way through the visitors – Anna Grigor'yevna, who had entered the room with him, standing somewhere to one side, apparently having taken a pair of opera-glasses – and he stepped on to the chair with one foot, eyes closed – or perhaps for that moment he was simply sightless – and then he placed his other foot on it: shoes sinking deep into the soft seat – and above the heads of the crowd, the painting could be seen to particular advantage, the Madonna floating in the clouds with the child in her arms, the apostle looking piously up at her from below, and the angels above – and this was the reason, all things considered, for standing up on the chair, because he did have to think of some explanation for the lackey who would try to drag him off – 'Fedya, are you mad!' – Anna Grigor'yevna stood beside him, looking up at him with startled eyes from below – even giving a discreet tug at his sleeve – and he was raised above all others – they were all pygmies, and one of the pygmies was rushing towards him – the attendant – and in place of the painting there appeared the face of the commandant with his bull-neck and Gargantuan chin, held in by the tightly fitting collar of his dress-uniform – smiling in a meek and even pleading sort of way, and not just the face, but there was his whole figure, strangely frail and cringing – and where the visitors had been, in place of their heads was a sea, and he and his wife swam into the deep-bluish distance, thrusting their arms up rhythmically, gulping in the air, moving further and further from the shore – and the prison commandant had nearly faded, his pitiful, bent figure scarcely visible somewhere in the distance, the figure of a beggar, asking for alms – 'Standing on chairs is forbidden in this gallery, sir,' – staring reprovingly at the well-dressed person standing on a chair, was the attendant, who then moved forward and lifted his arm as though offering support to the person on the chair, who stepped down, almost jumping, pushing aside the attendant's hand, and saw Anna Grigor'yevna standing in the corner of the room, having had time to move away and who was now pretending to be minutely examining a picture through her opera-glasses, but her hands, as she held the glasses, trembled – 'For heaven's sake, let's get away from here,' she said when he came up to her, her voice hoarse with agitation – visitors were looking round at them and whispering together about something – and taking him by the arm, she led him towards the door leading into the next room.

He should have remained standing on the chair to the bitter end, in spite of the lackey's reprimand, but he had given in and stepped down – appearing now in the wide window of the room, the commandant's face smiled contemptuously, and his fat, fleshy hand rakishly smoothed his moustache in a gesture of victory – and people stared through the guard-room windows, friends of the prisoner and women, too, their eyes full of pity and concern, and he lay across the table with his trousers down, and the guard methodically lashed him – Anna Grigor'yevna's arm was brusquely shaken away and, with lowered head, she resolutely walked into the next room – the chair should not have been left empty – it was unnatural, an empty chair – heading quickly for the centre of the room, his feet sinking again into something soft and springy – to stand as long as he liked now – to overcome in himself that humiliation in the face of a servant – could he never cross that boundary? – the crowd had fallen silent, as they do before the curtain rises – and the commandant's face, once again in the place of the painting, winked at him arrogantly – swinging his arm, he slapped his cheek, and the face disappeared, slumping probably with the rest of the commandant's body, which lay on the floor next to the polished table – the prisoner he had tried to punish standing in a triumphant pose, leg placed firmly on the commandant's stomach, and the audience staring in through the windows clapped him loudly, and the women, especially the intimate ones, looked at him with delight and blew him kisses – unhurriedly stepping from the chair – not jumping but carefully stepping – he headed deliberately towards the next room – in the doorway bumping into the attendant who it seemed had been out of the room somewhere, and the lackey politely let him pass.

That night, when he went to kiss Anya, they swam away

again together, rhythmically thrusting out their arms from the water and raising their heads to take in gulps of air – and the current did not sweep him away – they swam towards the receding horizon, into the unknown, deep-blue distance, and then he began to kiss her again – a dark triangle appeared, upturned – its apex, its peak, pointing downwards, forever inaccessible, like the inverted peak of a very high mountain disappearing somewhere into the clouds – or rather the core of a volcano – and this peak, this unattainable core, contained the answer both terrible and exquisite to something nameless and unimaginable and, throughout his life, even in his letters to her, he maintained the incessant struggle to reach it, but this peak, this core, remained forever inaccessible – and had he really stood on that chair for as long as he actually wanted to? – the attendant, after all, had been absent when he stood on it for the second time, so it could not be said he had been standing there in defiance of the attendant's will, even though he had resolved to remain in that position until he was led away – and if they had led him away, the attendant and maybe even a policeman – they would have dragged him across the whole room in full view of everyone including Anya, and everything would have thundered down as if from a high mountain – quickly, very quickly, and no longer could he have raised himself up from the polished table on which they had beaten him, and the commandant's face would have hung over him like a flushed red ball, like the gorged abdomen of a blood-sated mosquito, and his whole life would have become exquisite torment, because such humiliation was literally breathtaking – but neither thing had happened – he had stepped down – voluntarily, without waiting for the attendant to return – and he had not, in fact, brought the business to a scandalous conclusion – the triangle's forbidden peak, both hidden in the clouds and disappearing into the depths of the earth, perhaps to the very centre of the earth where the molten rock was constantly boiling, this peak had remained inaccessible.

Although Anya was gently stroking his face, he, without even saying his usual 'Goodnight', went off to his own room, and half an hour later she was woken by a strange sound –

one moment wheezing, the next gurgling – lighting the candle with trembling hands, she flew to her husband's bed – and he lay on the very edge, twisting his body as though he wanted to sit up but was prevented by an invisible rope which tethered him to the bed, face turning blue, mouth foaming – all her strength was used to drag him towards the middle of the bed so he would not fall and, kneeling down and taking a towel, she began wiping the foam from his lips and the sweat which poured from his forehead – and now he lay there peacefully, face as pale as a corpse – the invisible rope had won – he had failed to sit up – but was this really her husband? – this blue-faced man, trying to sit up in bed, fighting someone's invisible resistance, foam bubbling on his lips, dishevelled straggly beard somehow slipping to one side – was he really the person she had climbed up that narrow, steep, dark staircase to see, little more than half a year ago, adjusting her veil, her heart pounding in agitation, drowning the click of her heels, gasping with excitement and checking in her bag for the hundredth time, where she had placed the new pencils and the packet of writing paper (surely she hadn't lost them?) which she had just bought in Gostiny Dvor – cunningly arriving an hour earlier than her fellow student (also good at shorthand) because, from the moment she had discovered *he* needed a stenographer, her world had begun to sway and swirl – on a ship in the middle of a storm, a gigantic wave had swept all the rigging and even the handrails away, leaving only the mast – and all those on deck struggled to reach this mast and cling to it, so as not to be washed overboard into the sea, but only one person could manage it, and this one person had to be her.

He had met her in the entrance-hall, his head tilted slightly to one side as if examining some strange insect, and at another door appeared an untidy, petulant-looking young man – his stepson – who gave a haughty, arrogant smile which he repeated as she entered, with a scarcely perceptible nod – and *he* conducted her into a tiny room containing a desk, a small round table, a few chairs with faded upholstery and, sitting her down at the round table, began to dictate to her – not looking at her again that day, but spending the whole time walking up and down the room dictating in an unpleasant, muffled voice, and she was afraid to ask him to repeat anything, because she thought he would send her away immediately, and she had to hold out, to grasp the mast before anyone else – and, teetering and falling, she slowly but surely made headway.

After working for three or four days, she caught him staring at her with bright, searching eyes, and she had the fleeting thought that he wanted to come to her to say something or ask her something, but she firmly lowered her gaze, staring with exaggerated interest at her shorthand notes – almost grasping the mast, but she mustn't rush, she mustn't lose her balance at the last moment – closer and closer he came to her each time – no longer walking from one corner of the room to the other as at first, but around her, the circles narrowing each time, a spider closing in on a fly – and there was something exquisite and forbidden for both of them about these inexorably narrowing circles, something that took her breath away – but she would still rigorously, and even piously now, shut her eyes to avoid his gaze – she, who had spun this spider's web or, perhaps, they had spun it together – and the threads of the web began to bend and looked as if they might break at any moment – but this 'any moment' turned into the opening of the study door and the poking in of the stepson's head with his arrogant, haughty and accusing smile, so that the circles changed back to diagonals – from corner to corner – and the orator made an effort, quite beyond his strength, not to peer at the stenographer, and she would greet the stepson's appearance at the door with a glowering stare from under the brows – maybe the first appearance of that look to be seen in the photograph on the first page of her *Diary*.

Finally, this whole spider's web business ended the way in which it had to end: exquisitely the victim felt his sting, and she grasped the mast, clinging to it with her whole body, so that no wave could sweep her away, so that no-one else could grasp it in her place and then he told her everything – about his penal servitude, his epilepsy, his lack of money (at which she already guessed), the contract which would transfer to

Stellovsky all rights to publication of his works, if he failed to submit his new novel by the 30th of the month – he sat at the round table opposite her, offering tea and pretzels which he had chosen himself at the pâtisserie on Voznesensky Prospect – how he loved to buy sweetmeats, and here in Dresden, returning from the post-office or the gallery, he would buy all kinds of delicacies, the ones she liked, as well as berries and fruit – and from the window she could see him approaching the house, weighed down with purchases, parcels in both arms – and then down to wait for him by the door – how he loved her to come out and meet him and take the parcels from his hands – and how angry he was if she even slightly delayed – back in Saint Petersburg, opposite her at the round table, he would pour the tea himself and reveal all in a cracked voice – her gaze no longer lowered, she looked at him straight in the eye, and this gaze from under the eyebrows seemed to him to be clear and gentle, and no doubt it was, that gaze – as he now and again pulled at his beard and, getting up to go to fetch some more tea from the kitchen, found his legs moving in a strange kind of way, as if they were still bound in chains – and then he began to visit their home in Peski, and her mother would fuss about laying the table, and they once travelled together by horse-cab – he was giving her a lift somewhere – and at some cross-roads or other the driver suddenly checked the horses, and she jerked forward under her own momentum, and although it was clear she would not fall, he grasped her by the waist and even fleetingly embraced her, and she blushed – and then, after their wedding, they travelled to Moscow and stayed at the Hotel Dussot in a small room on the second floor with its view of the snow-covered bell-towers and cupolas of Moscow's churches and, down below, the white blanketed streets with their sledge-ploughed furrows – and most days, huddled in a warm fur blanket, off they set in a sledge, from the hotel, heading towards his sister on Staraya Basmannaya Street – stopping off on the way near the Menshikov Tower and then at the Church of the Assumption of the Virgin on the Pokrovka to walk briefly around the outside – he was showing her everything on her first visit to Moscow, as the owner of a house would display his prize possessions – stepping from the sledge, as they made for the church, he would stop for a moment, take off his hat, genuflect and cross himself, and she would do likewise.

And at his sister's she caught the hostile looks – they had wanted to marry Fedya to some relative, and it had not worked out – and she glowered back, but when Fedya left for another room or engaged the young ladies in lively conversation, the mast, to which she firmly clung, so firmly she almost forgot her arms were round it, this mast suddenly began to slip from her hands – lowering her eyes, pretending to adjust the flounces on her dress, her fingers – against her will – crumpled the fabric and, raising herself a little from the chair, she smoothed out the crinoline again – and in the hotel room, when the corridors were silent, he would come to her to say goodnight just as he did here in Dresden, and they began to swim, thrusting their arms from the water, and they swam so far that the coast began to disappear – and in Petersburg, hostile looks again from the stepson and Emiliya Fyodorovna, his late brother's wife, a shrunken lady with sharp, coal-black eyes, and all of them wanted to take him from her – and time and again creditors appeared at their flat, fat, self-satisfied merchants with thick gold rings on their short, fleshy fingers, with ornaments on heavy gold chains hanging down from their waistcoat pockets – all demanding payment for the debts owing on his brother's bankrupt tobacco factory and on both of the brothers' former publishing venture – endless negotiations – and then the district police-chief in his peaked cap with its light-blue band, announcing with a click of the heels an official inventory of their property to be taken the following day – and then she left for her mother's – and her mother made the sign of the cross over her and kissed her on both cheeks, saying she would pawn the family heirlooms – and they managed to pay off the creditors for the time being and avoid the sequestration of their goods and left Petersburg, going abroad to get as far away as possible from this whole nightmare, from the hostile looks, from the stepson, from the creditors – and when they sat down in the railway carriage, it seemed to her that a new life was beginning for the two of them.

He was lying down as before, having abandoned his attempts to sit up – his breathing still uneasy and irregular, hissing violently through his clenched teeth, turning to foam on his lips – and somewhere inside his throat, a bubbling, gurgling sound as if he were gargling – still kneeling in the same position beside him, she rubbed the foam and sweat away with a towel, as far as his forehead, pale like the rest of his face – she stared into his eyes – open, their gaze fixed on her, but he did not recognize her, and projected on the wall by the flickering light of the candle was the dancing shadow of his dishevelled beard, the shape of some shaggy monster – and sudden fear took hold of her, and she rushed to the door to call Mme Zimmermann or a servant, or the doctor, but then he called out to her quietly and clearly, and she knelt at his side again, staring into his eyes, stroking his forehead – and finding her other hand, he drew it towards him and pressed it to his lips – thirteen and a half years later, in exactly the same way, he drew her hand to his lips after she had read the passage chosen by him at random from the Gospels and he had summoned the children to bid his farewell – lying in his Petersburg apartment on a leather couch with its back beneath the photograph of the 'Sistine Madonna', the birthday gift, looking almost as Kramskoy pictured him, his head sinking slightly into the raised cushion, forming creases in it which seemed to radiate out from his head like rays of light, eyes closed, the expression on his face severe and yet peaceful – as is almost always the case with a corpse – and his long and strangely darkened beard, curling away like links on a chain.

I see a beard like that nearly every morning in the trolleybus – a beard belonging to an old man who steps cheerfully on at the stop beside a large, clean, two-storeyed detached house with curtains always drawn and a plaque on the wall saying 'Council of Ministers for the USSR, Committee for Religious Affairs' – an erect old man with a thick, gnarled walking-stick in his hand, and sporting an old-fashioned peaked cap, of the kind once worn by shopkeepers and others of that ilk (he had probably kept it from those days) – and his clothes are also out-of-date, a waistcoat over what looks like a traditional Russian shirt – everything well-worn, but clean and neat – and sitting down he places both hands on top of his stick, one over the other, and his hands are also well cared for and large – the expression on his face, pious and austere, his beard thrust slightly forward – and for some reason I avoid entering his field of vision, examining him on the sly – and he gets off at the same stop as I do, but heads past the Metro – walking quickly, leaving me behind – and goes round the corner towards the church where morning service is shortly due to begin.

The train began to rumble over the bridge and, tearing myself away from my book, I pressed my face against the window, cupping my hands to blot out the bright carriage light – and though it was still only evening, not even late evening, through the dim winter whiteness I could see a mass of lights flickering somewhere in the distance – and the doors began to slam at the end of the carriage as passengers with suitcases started to make for the exit, colliding with some children and young girls coming in, shaking dry the glasses and thermos-flasks in their wet hands, because there was either no towel in the lavatory or else it was too wet and dirty to use – the train was approaching Kalinin – outside you could make out the lights of the station and, somewhere beyond them, lines of street-lights disappearing into the distance, the glimmering level-crossing hut, the dipped headlights of cars waiting to cross the track, and another set of brighter lights, and then heaving slowly in sight directly below the window, the high flood-lit platform itself, snow-covered and dotted with figures in winter overcoats and sheepskins, suitcases in hand – and then the station building with its brightly lit windows framing yet more figures – in the restaurant, the waiting-room, at the ticket office, by the newspaper kiosk – and the train finally stopped just beyond the station building – and once again doors began to bang and clouds of frosty steam billowed from the door on to the platform where people were milling around – some running along in search of their carriage, others jumping coatless out of the train on the look-out for beer, pasties and newspapers – and on the other side of the platform sat an identical train with red carriages going in the other direction, from Leningrad to Moscow – Kalinin was their meeting place – and it was extremely easy, after rushing around buying pasties or newspapers, to confuse the two trains and head off in the wrong direction.

But somewhere beyond these two stationary, symmetrical trains, in the snowy darkness lit up only by the lines of occasional streetlights disappearing into the gloom, sprawled the buildings of this unknown city – and Dostoyevsky arrived here from Semipalatinsk, straight from exile, with his first wife, the consumptive and hysterical Mariya Dmitri-yevna – at first staying in a hotel and then, a few days later, moving into three furnished rooms near the post-office – autumn was just beginning, but soon the real season overtook them with its early evenings and late sunrises and its rains – he would spend his time rushing through a city drowning in mud, from one department to another – and then to the post-office to send requests and petitions to the Tsar with medical certificates appended begging for per-mission to live in Saint Petersburg – and then at night to meet his brother at the railway station en route from Petersburg to Moscow and then back again to meet him on the return journey – and then at night again over the three versts separating the station from the post-office if someone else were passing through Tver'* – and he was no longer young, this man with the skirts of his threadbare frock-coat fluttering, with his small, unnatural, dyed-looking moustache yet to be shaven off after his promotion to NCO for obedient behaviour – this man, darting from side to side, this way and that, meeting those arriving in Tver' from Moscow or Petersburg, bowing, shouting, demanding, clutching at the tailcoat folds or frock-coat skirts of highly-placed gentle-men, begging them to listen to what he had to say, pleading with them, cunningly calculating his moves so as not to sell

---

* The pre-revolutionary name for the city of Kalinin (Translators' Note).

himself short, not unlike those Jews who would later pester him and Anna Grigor'yevna in Vilna, offering their services, or tearfully entreating his brother in a letter to buy a hat for Mariya Dmitriyevna, and it had to be a violet one, because she couldn't just go around bare-headed and there was nothing to buy here.

Eleven years later he and Anna Grigor'yevna would make another visit to Dresden, living in the usual furnished flat at the corner of the building, because the corner was the apex of his eternal triangle – in the flat, on a desk with the traditional guttering candle and the glass of strong tea, there would appear one night the first notes written in tiny, almost calligraphic script and out of the mist began to emerge the figure of the Prince,* that principal antithesis to himself, that embodiment of his own unattainable dream, that demonic-faced superman, stepping firmly and with diabolical gait over the shaky wooden planks placed along one of the streets, drowning in a muddy nocturnal gloom, of the provincial capital where he settled after his period of exile – and next to Stavrogin, no, not next to him but behind him and walking through the mud itself because *next* to him and over the self-same planks he *dare* not go, came with tiny, mincing steps Pyotr Stepanovich Verkhovensky, speaking smoothly and quickly, cunning, obsequious and, if necessary, murderous, his greyish-looking face probably topped with close-cropped hair and a bald patch which reminds me strangely of a certain acquaintance of mine.

We were in the same class at school and you could even say that our families were good friends – my friend's father was often to be found at our house – mainly to visit my grandfather who was almost the same age, but this man had a weakness for women and was often changing wives (they were Russians, incidentally, and he himself was Jewish, of course) – he was, as I later found out, a third-rate pianist – an ordinary teacher at the Conservatoire or some music school – but at that time I, who had dabbled in composition myself,

---

* In the early versions of the novel *The Possessed* Stavrogin figures under the name of Prince. Stavrogin is also called 'Prince' by his crippled wife (Author's Note).

looked upon him as something mysterious and inaccessible, almost as God, and once – it happened only once, and that is why he became God to me beyond all question of doubt – once, having arrived at our flat, he sat down at the piano, opened the same lid which I used to open, touched the same keys on which I used to play my exercises and, sitting at our ordinary, everyday, slightly out-of-tune, upright piano which used to stand in the dining-room, he began to play a Chopin waltz – number seven, the waltz which I had tried vainly to learn by heart – and as his hands with their swollen, dark-blue veins began to soar, to fly up and down the key-board with the speed of swallows, I could feel a kind of exquisite lump in my throat and tears very likely even appeared in my eyes – and this man was small, lean and agile and died of heart-failure before the war (in the street, I think) even earlier than my grandfather, probably as a result of sensual excess – and his son, my classmate, the offspring of his last wife – a plump, simple, round-faced woman who, we used to say at home, looked like a cook or a maid (I don't think we even received her in our house, or perhaps he never brought her with him on visits) – my classmate was mischievous and lively like his father, from whom he had also inherited a very good ear, but he was contemptuous of music, was a bad pupil and, when he was fourteen or fifteen, left to join a flying-school – and then, after the war, I met him several times – he was fairly short, like his father, hair close cropped to make the bald patch in the middle of his head less obvious, very talkative, speaking quickly and very smoothly, already divorced, remarried and provided with children from the second marriage – but he would complain that his heart was shaky and that was why he no longer did any flying but worked either as an air-traffic controller or as a navigator at the airport in the city where we once lived – and when he found out once that I was passing, or rather, flying through, he came into the departure lounge to see me and then insisted on accompanying me as far as the 'plane, so that we were let through ahead of the queue, and the passengers waiting to board the 'plane stood respectfully to one side as we walked towards the metal gate leading to the

runway – and he walked beside me, small and dressed in civil
aviation worker's uniform with some incomprehensible
badges pinned to the lapels, holding a light-blue peaked cap
with a golden emblem, his face grey-looking, and with his
bald patch – rapidly telling me something about being fed up
with his work, how tired he was and how he would send the
whole lot of them to hell, his speech studded with swear-
words but in a particular way, not with any emphasis but as
an integral part of his discourse – and even when we were
children, when our two families had lived in neighbouring
summer dachas, he used to clamber over the fence, shouting:
'Hallelujah! Cock-sucker!' – or at least that was the story my
mother used to tell years later, and it is still the first thing she
remembers, whenever the conversation turns to my old
classmate.

Pyotr Verkhovensky was mincing along after Stavrogin
and then, I think, tried to grab him by the sleeve because he
needed to beg something from Stavrogin, but the Prince,
flashing his demonic eyes in the darkness, flung him to one
side – and in just the same way he flung Pet'ka the convict
aside as he lay in wait for him on the bridge one dark
stormy night and his eyes flashed as demonically as the knife
in Pet'ka's hand poised to stab the Prince to death – but with
a single movement the Prince tore it from Pet'ka's hands and
graciously handed it back – the Prince was returning from
Zarech'ye, from Lebyadkin's house after meeting the
crippled woman – and a few days later, perhaps even the
very next day, and in the middle of the night, during a
scandalous ball at the governor's house, that same Zarech'ye
would burst into flames (and was it not Zarech'ye I could see
in those flickering lights outside the carriage window?), and
people had raced to the fire straight from the ball and from
every other place in town, rushed there in crowds, as always
happens with fires – and Stavrogin, too, had arrived at the
fire with Liza, the current victim of his cold, calculating
passion – and the house (surely it couldn't have been
Lebyadkin's?) was encircled by flames, with the neighbouring
houses also ablaze, their red-hot wooden beams exploding
in all directions with a sharp cracking sound like Bengal

lights – and she had just surrendered to the Prince, about half an hour before, and, like all properly brought-up girls, was trembling and pale after the experience – and how the author and hero of *Notes from Underground* would grind his teeth and long for such conquests, and also the narrator of *The Insulted and the Injured*, and the hero of *White Nights* and, it goes without saying, Makar Devushkin – that agonizingly sweet, magical fire was almost the counterpoint of the novel and on the way to this counterpoint the Cathedral towered, on Cathedral Square, of course, and the Jew, Lyamshin, having broken the glass, let a mouse in behind the covering of the icon of Our Lady of Kazan' placed in the wall next to the main entrance to the Cathedral, and the next day all the well-brought-up citizens of the provincial capital walked up to the Cathedral, stood a long while and then, nodding their heads in silent accusation, went their separate ways – but the important thing was that they said nothing – no doubt an expression of the great forbearance of Russian Orthodoxy and even of its messianic destiny – and the Jew, Lyamshin, certainly knew how to entertain the guests when his 'fellow countrymen' gathered together, deftly playing on the piano, mimicking geese, pigs and various respectable personages (probably even the governor), and generally clowning around and making a fool of himself – but after the fire, at the moment of the greatest counterpoint, the murder one foul autumn evening of Shatov in a distant, gloomy part of Stavrogin's park near a cave by the bank of the pond – he collapsed in hysterics, howling wildly and then spent the whole of the next day trembling with fear, refusing to emerge from under his blanket, pretending to be ill and hoping somehow to deceive people – and the figure of the person who only yesterday was still in exile and who had just returned from Semipalatinsk with his dyed-looking moustache and frock-coat flapping in all directions, darted this way and that, clutching at the flaps and lapels of full-dress uniforms and tail-coats with decorations and orders, begging, pleading, demanding, cunningly trying to secure the right of residing in Petersburg and continuing his literary career.

I once stood near that cave which is actually not in Tver', but in Moscow in the grounds of the former Petrovsko-Razumovskoye, and now the Timiryazev All-Union, Agricultural Academy, by a pond, or rather a lake, or rather an artificial reservoir, one of a whole series there now with diving-towers and boating-stations – small craft ploughing the waters of these lakes in various directions with affectedly hearty and high-pitched shrieks emanating from within – the place full of young people from the Timiryazev district of Moscow out for a walk or for entertainment or simply to get a sun-tan – and in the midst of this summer day a dark violet storm-cloud suddenly materialized, covering the sky, the wind started to blow, and the boats immediately began to moor at the boating-stations, while the people sunning themselves in the park hurriedly dressed to rush home – the ground above the cave where some noisy youths had been playing ball, also became deserted – the cave had columns and an iron grille to prevent people from entering, but in the darkness deep inside there was enough light to see the traces of human occupation, the grille obviously not doing its job – the two sloping sides of the cave had coarse gravel scattered beneath them to give the place a more decorative appearance – and in the almost twilight darkness I even fancied that I could hear the tops of the trees sounding as they did on that autumn evening when Shatov was murdered and Lyamshin was convulsed in hysterics, clutching at the clothes of the people surrounding the murdered man and uttering such terrible cries that he had to be tied up and to have some sort of gag stuffed into his mouth.

The first drops of rain began to fall, the violet cloud was torn by lightning, there was a clap of thunder, and I, too, was running down the avenue as quickly as I could, heading for the exit to the park to try and shelter from the approaching thunderstorm – and in one of those columned buildings facing the street and backing on to the park that Anna Grigor'yevna's brother had probably lived in as a student at the Petrovsko-Razumovskoye Academy – she had visited him on one of the days spent with her husband in Moscow immediately after their wedding when they stayed at the

Hotel Dussot and would visit her sister-in-law on Staraya Basmannaya Street in the evenings, when Anna Grigor'yevna would sit on a chair, eyes lowered, trying with exaggerated effort to smooth out the folds in her dress and the mast to which she clung seemed to be slipping from her hands – and her brother, according to her own description, had an open, prepossessing appearance – young, rosy-cheeked, fair-haired, cheerful: the very picture of Russian health – she spent longer at his place than the agreed time because an unending stream of students kept calling in at the room where he lived, all eager to meet the wife of the author of *Crime and Punishment*, or that at least was her story, and the servant was bringing in one samovar after another – and all this time Fedya waited at the crossroads near the Hotel Dussot in the dark of a winter's evening which had already fallen as she sat at her brother's, peering at the figures of women passing by in taxi-cabs – so no-one can be sure whether he even saw that cave or not.

The train had started long before, leaving the lights of Kalinin flickering in the snowy darkness somewhere behind it – gathering speed, it began to lurch more and more from side to side so that I had to hold on to the book to prevent it slipping on to the floor – there was a train in the book, too, a train with carriages of a kind I have never seen, low-slung like the foreign ones which travel to Budapest or Belgrade bearing the inscription 'Vagon Letti', not metal carriages but wooden ones with a large number of doors, each leading into a separate compartment with two soft, plush-covered settles placed opposite each other – rocking gently in time with the piston strokes in the engine as the train galloped along as fast as a troika of post-horses – with three people to each settle, gentlemen and ladies with round cardboard boxes on their laps and travelling-bags in the luggage-racks above them – the men wearing top-hats and carrying walking-sticks, the ladies dressed in tall, veiled, wide-brimmed, feathered hats and travelling shawls – and when Fedya disappeared somewhere for a moment, some German Fritz, travelling with his aged sister and very kind towards her, sat down in his seat and refused to give it up because, as

26

he insisted, Fedya had placed his things not on the seat itself, as he ought to have done so that everyone could see the place was taken, but up on the luggage-rack – and Fedya came back and announced that *he* was not going to give up his seat, but sat down next to the window for the time being in the old woman's seat, for some reason unoccupied (perhaps she had left the compartment) – the guard was summoned – the German went red, as all Germans do when angry or discomfited, and pronounced that it was '*recht*' and still refused to give the seat up – but then for some unknown reason sat down in another seat next to Anna Grigor'yevna and squirmed about so much that they all changed seats again, with the result that finally everyone was satisfied.

The Dostoyevskys were travelling from Dresden to Baden-Baden where Fedya intended to win a large sum of money at roulette to pay off his debts – having already been on a trip more than once to Bad Homburg, leaving Anna Grigor'yevna in the care of Mme Zimmermann, who once went as far as accompanying Anna Grigor'yevna on a steamship down the Elbe, but Anna Grigor'yevna was spending more and more time wandering about alone, inspecting old castle ruins and running off several times a day to the post-office or to meet the train, but Fedya continued to delay his return and wrote that he would be staying there yet another day and asked her to send him some money – she could still get around fairly easily, although she would sometimes feel sick, and just before his departure they had talked about their future Misha or their future Sonya, the names already firmly decided – but the day before he was due to return from Bad Homburg she had accidentally, or perhaps not accidentally, opened a letter addressed to him from the woman in whose company he had visited these same places a few years earlier as well as Italy and Paris later on, also to play roulette – and that woman's name was the one given to the main heroine of *The Gambler*, dictated to herself during the first month of their acquaintance – she had tried then to write as fast as she could and, sitting up till late at night at her own place, had copied it all out in time for him to read through in the morning – and it all had to be completed before the month was out so as not to be subject to Stellovsky, and thanks to her help he had managed to finish it on time and avoid this enslavement.

Mlle Polina was an unattainable woman, of course, particularly notable both for her aristocratic manners and for her ability not to notice things, for a kind of wounded, morbid pride and also for her strength of character – whereas Anna Grigor'yevna's pencils would always break, and she could feel herself blushing whenever he looked at her, and she would clumsily crumple the flounces on what was almost a schoolgirl's skirt, and her voice would fail her whenever he asked her about anything, and just at that moment his stepson would look in at his study, carelessly dressed, his naked chest showing beneath his dirty shirt – all greasy somehow, and then there was that arrogant smile of his – and Polina at this time hovered above at a terrible, unattainable height, and he was on his knees before her, ready to kiss the soles of her boots – and now here *she* was again, not in a novel this time, but in the flesh, her actual handwriting, unknown to Anna Grigor'yevna before now – and she could feel the mast beginning to slip away from her hands once again as she paced up and down the room, her hands clutching her temples, as if she had migraine or had to solve some urgent problem – and the other one had called *her*, Anna Grigor'yevna, Brylkina in the letter, although her surname had been Snitkina, and this confusion of two not completely dissimilar names was something particularly insulting and contemptuous, as if the whole world contained only Polina – by herself, the main person – and Anna Grigor'yevna was some petty obstruction in her path, not deserving serious attention, like a dirty puddle or muddy patch which could quite easily be avoided – and she placed the letter on his desk amongst all the others, as if it were of no greater significance, and when she met him at the station at last and they set off home, he took her carefully by the arm, gazing at her intently as if trying to discover any changes which had occurred during his absence – and while they walked along like this, in step with each other, he with his travelling-bag in hand and face covered with smuts of soot from the journey, and she with her mind on how they would arrive home any minute and how she would begin to wash and iron his linen – while they walked along like this, she somehow managed to forget the letter, but when he sat down at his desk and began to sort through his mail, she stood with her back pressed tightly to the jamb of the door, gripping it from behind with her hands as if she might fall over (she had to see his reaction to it with her own eyes) – and he opened the letter and immediately the whole of his body seemed somehow to spring forward.

Having arrived in Paris he had gone immediately to visit her in her hotel – and she had come out to meet him in a long dress and with a heavy, dark-brown plait entwined around her head – and he fell down at her feet, because he had already seen from her eyes that something had happened, and she declared to him, as people do only in novels, that she had fallen in love with another man, a handsome Spaniard, the mannequin type, with jet-black hair flowing over his shoulders, deep-blue eyes and blindingly white teeth, a pampered aristocrat or, to be honest, a run-of-the-mill playboy, who had already discarded her – but *he* was in a state to accept anything, and he begged her to go away with him – so they stayed in adjacent hotel rooms, they travelled together on trains, they occupied the same steamer cabin, but they made a vow to each other just to remain *friends* – or rather he suggested this himself, for otherwise she would never have agreed to travel with him, and he knew in advance the absurdity of the idea, obscurely hoping and believing in the depths of his soul that something else would happen, and this something, although it never occurred in reality, would nevertheless appear in his dream – and then they would swim away together towards the distant blue horizon, thrusting up their arms evenly and rhythmically, breathing a single breath: his breath was her breath – but, on waking, he found himself slumped on the shore in an uncomfortable position and she was nowhere in sight – perhaps she had vanished beyond the horizon, perhaps she had never even entered the water, and he would rush into her room without knocking, hoping against hope – and encounter her dressed in her morning peignoir, graciously offering him her hand like a queen – and catching sight of her unmade bed and closing his eyes for a moment, he imagined himself swimming with her once again, but the Italian sun mercilessly forcing its way through the loosely drawn curtains and the lively voices of street-traders and the sound of carriages from outside ended the morning with nothing – and the whole day lay ahead, filled with the same merciless sun – and even more agonizing were the shipboard journeys in the same cabin when, at night, he would wake from his dreams and, in the twilight before dawn, could make out the contours of her body beneath the light downy quilt – and once, after throwing on his dressing-gown, he sat down on the bed beside her – and slightly raising her head, awash with her hair, she tried to push him away, but he pressed himself against the quilt which covered her knees and began to kiss it – and she threatened to call the servants, and he somehow slipped to find himself sitting on the rug beside the bed – and the boat was rocking slightly and the sound of seagulls floated in through the port-hole – on deck and in the restaurant people took them for lovers – and he kissed the edge of the sheet which had slipped off the bed – 'You have gone mad!' she screamed – she was leaning back on the bed-head with hair spread everywhere and eyes wide open with fear, like the painting of Princess Tarakanova, as if at any moment water might flood into the cabin* – and seeing the fear in her eyes, he kissed the rug which lay on the floor – and everything seemed to be tumbling downhill, out of control, and the feeling of falling took his breath away – and he needed her to walk over him – because he had to crash at the bottom somehow – and he saw himself from the side – lying face down in the night on the cabin floor, wearing a dressing-gown, no longer young, with foam on his lips, and he must have briefly blacked out for the foam to be there at all.

His hands trembled a little as he held the letter and read

---

* A reference to Konstantin Flavitsky's painting of 1864 depicting the adventuress known as the Princess Tarakanova dying in her cell at the Peter-Paul Fortress in Petersburg during the great flood of 1777 (Translators' Note).

the lines written in her hand – and Anna Grigor'yevna clutched the door-jamb so hard it hurt her fingers, and she thought that at any moment the room would begin to sway and she would fall.

The train was speeding along a narrow track twisting capriciously between round-topped hills covered by dark-green forests of beech, elm and other native trees of the plains and uplands of Central Germany – Schwarzwald, Thüringer Wald and all the other mountain areas – a toy train made up of tiny little carriages and a miniature steam-engine with red spokes on its wheels and a tall chimney, the sort you see nowadays on special stamps depicting the history of locomotives – and in one of the carriages of this doll's train, in a second-class compartment, was seated a man no longer young, in a dark suit obviously made in Berlin, with plain Russian face, receding temples and greying brown beard – and next to him was a youngish woman, not unlike a student but with heavy, glowering gaze, wearing a hat and travelling shawl and with a cardboard box on her lap – and sometimes she would begin to doze off, leaning her head against her husband's shoulder while he, squinting his eyes, would carefully and suspiciously inspect her face, as if trying to read something.

I saw him recently at an exhibition of paintings by a popular artist – in the top left-hand corner of a picture being looked at by so many people that the lower half of the painting was concealed from where I stood – but managing to push my way through even so, I then saw what I had expected to, after hearing reports from other people – three plump hogs, very pink and slightly unreal, exactly the sort of animals seen in posters showing the champion workers at a pig farm, and a little way beyond, or rather, above the pigs lay some corpse, either blood-stained or beheaded – and a little above that – high enough to be seen at a distance without having to push forward – was a long table littered with the remains of a feast, with goblets containing some heavy, red liquid supposedly representing blood – and a little higher still, to the left, even closer to the author of *The Possessed*, in front of a dark-haired man strangely embodying

31

a mixture of industrial shockworker and primitive muzhik, knelt a barefoot, bare-chested youth with identical features, dressed only in jeans – and further left, at the top, above a semi-circular line apparently meant as a kind of halo, the sort usually seen suspended over a saint, was a clustering throng of distinguished Russians: Lomonosov and Peter the Great wearing wigs, Saltykov-Shchedrin, Lev Tolstoy and various others including the author of *The Possessed* – all of them incorporeal somehow, with pale features, as though they had slipped from the pages of a pile of school textbooks – and the painting was called 'The Return of the Prodigal Son', and next to it was a small notice on which was explained, in large type to avoid any possible misunderstanding, exactly what the artist had intended to express in his work – and the crowd was besieging this painting which took up half the wall, so that it was not so much a picture as a whole sheet of canvas, almost like the 'Appearance of Christ to the People' – and behind the crowd lurked a few men with simple faces – the sort who might be seen playing dominoes – and one of them, obviously tipsy, his pocket bulging probably with a half-litre bottle of vodka, was ranting on at everyone, gesticulating wildly and jabbing his finger towards the painting – and I suddenly thought of the heels of Rembrandt's Prodigal Son falling at his father's feet, as I looked at the heels of the kneeling youth in jeans looming indistinctly, the central focus of the painting.

The toy train, enveloped in clouds of smoke puffed out by the tall chimney of its engine, continued on its meandering journey between Schwarzwald and Thüringer Wald – you could almost pick it up in your hands along with all its little carriages and passengers, as Gulliver did with the inhabitants of Lilliput, and you could imagine putting all these little people on top of a table to watch them walk about and then enjoy the fun as you blow on them, as you might blow out a candle – and what a commotion there would be during this hurricane, like ants when a stick or even a simple match is poked into their ant-hill.

As she woke up and looked out of the window, Anna Grigor'yevna could see the dark-green vegetation covering the hills and mountains, their peaks or spurs appearing white, red or pink, depending on the light, the colour of the stone, and the time of day, and former imperial castles with their crenellated towers, just as she had imagined them from the pictures hanging in their drawing-room – and from those dark forests covering the slopes of the mountains, fairy-tale dwarfs would emerge playing on reed-pipes – and from slope to slope would reverberate those syncopated, triple-measured Tirolean yodels with their modulations, their reprises, like mountain echoes – and at the foot of the hills would ripple peaceful German streams with herds of fat cattle and sheep grazing in their pastures – and towns would sail by with their red-roofed, sharp-gabled houses and Gothic towers, the inhabitants strolling at leisure through the streets, their heavy, lace-up boots resounding against the cobble-stones.

Anna Grigor'yevna and Fedya had changed trains several times – sometimes during the day, sometimes at night – and Fedya would accompany Anna Grigor'yevna to the ladies' room because she felt nauseated, and in one place was even sick – Leipzig, Naumburg, Erfurt, Eisenach, Frankfurt – in Frankfurt they booked in at a hotel a couple of steps from the station, ordered themselves veal cutlets and soup and then went to inspect the city – and walked into Lange Strasse, a big avenue with trees bearing white blossom – and a German told them that it was white acacia – and Anna Grigor'yevna liked the trees very much – she had never seen them in flower before – then they found themselves in a big street not unlike Nevsky Prospect with a large number of shops – and they bought a very expensive copy of Herzen's *Bell* – fifty-four kreutzers – and then Fedya chose a cravat – a pink one with a pattern of little rings which cost three florins fifteen kreutzers – but the shop had no suitable scarf for Anna Grigor'yevna, because they were either too narrow or too wide or were just not particularly nice-looking – and in one shop they had a look at some very nice hats because Fedya kept repeating that Anna Grigor'yevna needed a new one – then they entered some long, hot street almost deserted at this hour with windows nearly all shuttered, making the city look dead – down some side-streets to emerge on the banks of the Main which looked so astonishingly like the picture of it hanging in the drawing-room of Anna Grigor'yevna's house – and then returning to the street resembling Nevsky, they entered yet another shop, Anna Grigor'yevna buying herself a lilac-coloured scarf for two florins twelve kreutzers and trying on a straw hat with lilac-coloured velvet, very pretty, which had taken her fancy as they walked down the street past this shop for the first time, but she dared not ask Fedya to go in then because he was so impatient to rush here, there and everywhere – and the price turned out to be twenty florins – simply scandalous, compared to Dresden – but in spite of this Fedya, with a bow, indicated to the French woman showing them the hat that they would buy it, suggesting she must be taking them for simpletons, for savages – and she replied in an extremely condescending way that, of course, they were obviously not savages and kept on repeating in broken Russian, *kho-ro-sho* ('good'), which finally made Fedya lose his temper completely and snap out a sharp rejoinder – and they left the shop without buying the hat after all and started walking along the streets once again – and then into a flower shop, spending a long time choosing roses because none of them was particularly nice – in the end buying a couple of roses after all, paying eighteen kreutzers for each of them.

Outside the carriage, through the morning mist which had yet to disperse, appeared the environs of Baden-Baden – Anna Grigor'yevna was dozing, her head on her husband's shoulder, as he glanced sideways at her face, examining it carefully and suspiciously – did this woman really love him? – that first time he had seen her at his house it had seemed unbelievable that this young woman, scarcely old enough to have left school, with fresh, innocent face slightly glowing from the street, would stay in his house forever, becoming his wife, and that he would have the right, at any time, to go up to her and kiss the back of her neck in the place where her hair was pinned up – but that very thought, that she might become his wife, had for some reason entered his head the very first time she sat in his study at a little round table, diligently taking down in shorthand the words he dictated in his muffled voice – and he had been purposely dry and sharp with her that day, so she would not feel the power she had already gained over him, but when, as he dictated to her, he imagined himself kneeling before her beneath the flickering light of a nearly spent candle and kissing her feet, with her unable to leave because she was his wife, and about to blow out the candle so they could plunge into the passionate, exquisite swim, then his voice became hoarse and he shut his eyes to blot out the sight of this little girl, as he purposely tried to picture her to help restrain his imagination, girl students being as untouchable as postulants – and did she really love him? – sometimes he thought she was simply pretending (hadn't just his name really attracted her?) – once, as he took aim in a Dresden shooting-gallery with her at his side, half-smiling, thinking he would not hit the target, she said to him: 'You'll miss' – and beforehand some German had hit the bull's-eye every time, making the iron figure of a Turk pop up from the floor – and she had been full of admiration, watching this German shoot, and the German had been flashing her significant looks – but all she said to *him* was: 'You'll miss' – and, just to show her, he hit the bull the very first time, and the iron Turk in his painted fez popped up off the floor just as he had done for the German – and turning round towards her in triumph, he said loudly, almost shouting: 'Well? Did I get the bull's-eye or not?' – and after each successful shot he turned round again to shout: 'Well?!' – so that people began to look round – and the expression on her face after each bull's-eye and each triumphant exclamation became more and more fearful and somehow pathetic, and this egged him on even more, and he bawled out his 'Well?' even louder with people beginning to cluster around them, and her face – each time he turned to fling his triumphant 'Well?' at her – was becoming more unlovely, and her forehead began to take on a kind of sallow tone – and at these moments he longed for her to grow old quickly and become plain and ugly like that, so that men like that German would stop casting looks at her and she would lose her power over him – in the letters she wrote to her relations she probably made fun of him, even ridiculing their swimming together – and sometimes she would pretend that she had not been sleeping, but he knew she had been asleep: he could tell by the sound of her voice – why couldn't she spend that half hour, when thoughts came to him so easily, sitting beside him at his desk? – but she would always disappear into the other room, and he knew for certain that she was asleep, but when he went in and shook her by the shoulder to rouse her, she immediately tried to assure him that she had been awake, although her eyes could not keep open – and this obvious lie infuriated him more than anything else – and this woman who simply did not want to sit with him, could engage in lively conversation with that garrulous and empty-headed German, Mme Zimmermann, about this and that kind of lace and other such trivialities – and once, after she was caught out sleeping yet again, pretending as always to have been awake, she came to his study after all and sat next to his desk – and he could feel, although he did not look, that her eyes could hardly stay open and that she was having to make a real effort – but he did not need *her* favours! – and the hooves of a cab-horse could be heard outside clattering by over the cobblestones, and somewhere over the sharp-gabled roofs of the red-brick buildings the sun was setting – and his train of thought kept shifting to something else, and he thought that this something else must be her, as she sat there not of her own accord, but compelled to – and then, jumping out of his chair, he began to shout that she was sitting there out of revenge, on purpose, to annoy him, and the more he realized the absurdity of this, the more angrily he shouted – let everyone hear what he had to say, especially that wonderful Mme Zimmermann, her intimate, her friend! – kicking the chair abruptly away he started to look for his *papirosas* – his hands trembled – and covering her face with her hands, Anna Grigor'yevna ran from the room, as he furiously flung about the books and papers on his desk and banged open all the drawers – and there was no sign of *papirosa* tubes although he remembered placing them near the right-hand edge of the desk so they would always be to hand – and running after her, knowing that the *papirosas* were a pretext, he found her sitting on the edge of the bed, her hands still covering her face, her shoulders trembling – and he knelt down in front of her and forced her hands away – tears were flowing down her face – and he started to kiss her hands and feet – she drew his head towards her and suddenly burst out laughing – and disentangling his head from her hands, he gazed questioningly into her eyes which were laughing and still moist with tears – and she said that she was laughing because people asleep were not accountable for their actions, but that was exactly what he demanded of her.

That evening, as always, he came to kiss her goodnight, and they swam so far that the coast disappeared from view as though it had never existed – on they swam, breathing rhythmically, plunging into the water, now thrusting themselves slightly out again to gulp air into their lungs – and when it seemed that the swimming would never end and that they would break free at any moment, no longer swimming but soaring lightly and easily over the water like seagulls, he suddenly remembered her laughing face – *of course* she had been laughing at him, and a counter-current pulled him to one side, and next to her face appeared the bloated features of the commandant, with his chin hanging down like a balloon, and this balloon seemed to bulge with blood like a mosquito's abdomen – and around these arrogantly grinning features appeared more faces – his friends and acquaintances, particularly women, including the one who had shared his cabin and whom he had dared not touch, and also the very first woman he had seen at the Vielgorskys' salon, where writers would gather in his younger days, before his arrest – so beautiful, so impossibly unattainable in her long dress with its silent train gliding after her as if she were a queen, so impossibly unattainable with her blond ringlets framing her face and the subtle fragrance of her perfume, that when she gave him her hand and held it fleetingly in his so that he would realize he must kiss this hand showing white through the slit of her glove, he staggered oddly and nearly fell – probably having briefly blacked out – the first harbinger of his illness? – and then everyone had laughed at him, and someone even wrote an offensive quatrain about him – but she remained just as serious and attentive towards him, simply taking her hand away – but now she, too, was beginning to laugh at him, and the others in the drawing-room were now really roaring with laughter, those self-satisfied mediocrities, glowing and engorged, those he had bared his soul to at that time – and they spread the tale all over Petersburg with little jokes and witty rhymes – and to think that he had imagined they drank in his every thought and worshipped *him*! – and now they were simply convulsed, and here he was already floundering near the shore, and Anya was swimming far away, almost at the horizon itself where the deep-blue of the sea merged with the identical blue of the sky – all of them, including her, laughed at him – and leaving her still swimming beyond the horizon, he threw on his dressing-gown, went into the other room, lit a candle and sat at his desk, burying his head in his hands – yes, she was his natural enemy, there was no doubt about it, and the next day, when she carelessly moved the table with their morning coffee, hurting him with its leg, he accused her of doing it on purpose – and then in the days which followed he told her several times that she was spiteful and unpleasant to him on purpose – and her face on these occasions would take on that pathetic, fearful expression it had worn in the shooting-gallery, and she no longer dared laugh but simply lowered her head further and further, as if trying to hide her face from him, and he would go down on his knees in front of her, kissing her feet and begging her to forgive him but, above all, not to laugh at him – and then, annoyed by this self-inflicted humiliation, he would jump to his feet and walk quickly up and down the room, diagonally from corner to corner, kicking away any chairs in his path and shouting out that he was still worthy of respect, even if he didn't have any money – and she would bow her head even lower, pressing her hands against it, as if she had migraine, and stand there motionless with a stony expression replacing the look of fear.

The familiar environs of Baden-Baden with their houses and country cottages were slowly passing by the window, but he continued to examine her face with the same rapt attention as she slept with her head resting on his shoulder, and for a moment he thought that her forehead and cheeks were taking on the sallow tone once again which he had noticed that time in the shooting-gallery – she was breathing peacefully and evenly – but, of course! she needed more sleep now and the sallowness was probably caused by the future Misha or Sonya! – how come he hadn't thought of this before? – and he stroked her head, rousing her, and she stared at him as children do when they have just awoken – 'We're arriving,' he told her – and beyond the carriage window she could see a high verdant mountain with white and red brick houses – and here and there the Gothic towers of churches, and above everything the deep-blue sky with fluffy clouds floating across it – just as she had imagined the city would be, but she had to get ready to get off the train and pack up their things.

He was leaning slightly back against the settle with his hands on his knees, as he would sit whenever he was being photographed, and was peering out at the approaching city – and through the garden vegetation covering the slopes of the mountain he had a clear view of a white, two-storeyed building with a Gothic roof whose windows, even during the daytime, were darkened by closed heavy velvet curtains – and suspended from the ceilings would be enormous crystal chandeliers lighting up the green-draped halls, their gloomy corners obscured by tobacco smoke, and in the middle of each hall – the large central one and the two slightly smaller side-rooms – stood tables, also covered with green cloth and surrounded by figures of people, their faces yellow from lack of sleep, their hands reaching for the tables littered with golden coins – and these gleamed with a kind of flickering reddish light like the covers of icons during a church-service when all the candles are lit and their flames glimmer in the clouds of incense – and in the very centre of the tables, rising above the scattered heaps of gold, were shimmering discs, green and red, and these were the altars, no less, or perhaps the royal gates, being accessible only to one person who sat there impassively and calmly performed mysteries over these sacred discs engraved with figures as black as agate or red as rubies, and spinning around in the middle of them, deciding the fate of one of the people standing round the table, was an elusive little silver sphere – as elusive as the ball in a game of tennis – and the golden coins scattered over the table would seem to collect themselves in piles as if an invisible hand had begun to sort them out and arrange them together – and the man seated in the train with his hands on his knees, closed his eyes – and many times he had won great heaps of these golden coins, but as soon as he reached out to gather them towards him, another hand had moved to grasp them, to rake them in – and this hand had belonged to one of those yellow faces crowding around the table, and he suddenly realized why these piles of coins always fell to them: they had no summit, of course – he had tried to take them before they formed the shape of a triangle – he had to wait until this shape, this summit was formed, and then that money would belong to him.

He opened his eyes as the train began to slow – and outside, the neat red-brick building of the station at Baden-Baden gradually floated into view and then stopped – and pressing her face to the window, Anna Grigor'yevna examined the station-building and the figures of the people pacing up and down the platform, as if someone were supposed to be meeting them there – Baden-Baden, the real, living thing, and she could already see herself walking with her husband down the Lichtenthaler Allee, the main street in Baden-Baden about which she had heard so much, surrounded by other visitors, all dressed in their smartest clothes – she had changed her black lace shawl for a magnificent flounced dress because at long last Fedya must be about to have some luck.

Once again, as in Dresden, they rented rooms from some ordinary German woman who ran a boarding-house with a chambermaid by the name of Marie, a very lively and swarthy girl who looked Italian – Anna Grigor'yevna put her at about fourteen years old – she looked so much like a child – but it turned out that she was eighteen – a cheerful girl, always laughing and emitting a raucous '*Ja*' which echoed throughout the house, but also amazingly stupid, as,

40

incidentally, all Germans are, male or female – she could never seem to understand right away what anyone said to her, and if something were repeated a hundred times over, she was still unable to comprehend (she would never provide a tablespoon at lunch – what ignorance!) – and in the courtyard of the house where they lodged was a smithy where hammering started up at four in the morning, and in the rooms next door to them children cried, long and hard, but all the same those first days of their stay in Baden-Baden were like a fine summer morning when you are hurrying out somewhere: rain has come during the night and everything has been washed clean – the grass, the asphalt, the houses and the trams, gleaming red as though they had just been freshly varnished – and you walk along impatiently as if expecting something unusual to happen, some great event which absolutely must take place today.

So it was when I was still a young student at the Institute – I would walk out of the hospital building where we lived during the years immediately following our evacuation, because the city we returned to had been practically destroyed and we were given a room in the hospital where my father worked, next to a latrine and a bathroom – the hospital building was old with extremely thick walls and smoke-blackened, vaulted ceilings – and before the Revolution it had been either an infirmary for impoverished Jews or a hospital for the elderly and infirm – and with crutches tapping on the stone floor, soldiers disabled in the last war would hobble past our door on the way to the latrine, dragging their legs along in their dirty plaster casts – and in the mornings when I would be rushing off to the Institute, I would pass through the tiny hospital garden where the invalids already ambled or sat on benches at wooden tables, rolling their own cigarettes out of newspaper, smoking or playing dominoes – and I quickly headed for the exit so as to reach the street outside as soon as possible – the street led uphill with only a few buildings left standing on it and bomb-sites in between, overgrown with grass and stinging nettles and piled with old bricks left over from the buildings that used to grace it – and nurses and even various doctors would greet me, because my father was the leading surgeon at the hospital, and the watchman at the gate would do the same – and I was already walking up the street, hurrying to the place where the varnished red trams ran, usually a single car, rarely with another coupled on – and the streets they travelled along could only tentatively be called streets as, stretching out on both sides of the tramline, were bomb-sites strewn with fragments of brick, overgrown with nettles, interspersed with buildings which by some miracle had survived, or simply with empty shells of houses, with torn strips of wallpaper hanging down and fluttering slightly in the wind or a tap or tiled Dutch stove sticking out somewhere about the level of the second floor – I was already moving onwards as quickly as possible to the tram which would take me to the Institute – past the buildings of a clinic situated on the outskirts of the town – like the hospital, having survived the war (the Germans tried specially to spare hospital buildings in order to make use of them themselves) – and the wind blew in through the half-opened window of the tram – I sat on a seat beside it facing the front of the tram – my favourite position in public transport (and I'm not the only one, I'm sure) – peering ahead of me, pressing my face to the window, sometimes even standing up for a moment and craning out, being extremely careful not to let any dust get in my eyes, and not to be struck by a telegraph pole – I could not yet make out the building I was heading for, but in the common-room or in the corridor male and female students in white lab-coats would be clustering around one of the junior doctors, and amongst them would be the girl with golden hair escaping from under her cap, the one-and-only girl who exists for all of us at that age, and for some of us not only then, the one-and-only girl both imaginary and at the same time real with fine blue veins in her temples beneath the delicate, tender skin and a heart rhythmically contracting to pump fresh, hot blood (is it really hot?) around the fragile, tensile arteries, as yet unsullied by a single nodule or grain of calcium, blood which gives the skin and the whole body that amazing pink tone termed flesh-coloured and which they all attempt to imitate with stockings and tights – wallpaper and lamp-shades are sometimes that colour, too, but never very successfully: only the skin of a young woman possesses that exact tone – and as I sit there in the tram, I try in mind to place myself next to that golden-haired student in such a position that the hair tumbling out from under her cap touches my cheek – and why is it only now in our declining years that we become so sensitive to the touch of a woman's hair and, sitting on public transport, surreptitiously try to let our cheek or bald patch brush against a cascade of female hair flooding down from somewhere? – and the more casual the touch, the stronger the feeling of contentment, as we can then, having purposely placed our skin against this cascade, try to convince ourselves that it is pure accident, and the more painful is the enforced parting from this cool golden flood pouring down from on high, heedlessly flowing over shoulders covered by a suede or denim jacket and transferring a charge of electrons to our ageing skin – and to receive this mysterious electron charge from some unwitting donor, and for that reason particularly desired, we, as we leave home in the morning, are also hurrying somewhere, filled with anticipation and certainty that something unusual must be about to happen to us, although at our age we ought rather to expect a thrombosis, but we still hurry as much as our heart, our obesity and our shortness of breath will allow.

During the first part of their stay in Baden-Baden Fedya actually happened upon a lucky streak, and Anna Grigor'-yevna's money-pouch or 'little sack' as she refers to it in one place, which had contained eighty coins on their arrival, began to bulge, and after a week and a half contained one hundred and eighty coins or 3000 francs – and Fedya would oscillate between the boarding-house and the Kurhaus where the roulette was, sometimes several times a day, now losing, now winning, but more often the latter – and he would lose on the whole by accident, when he was pushed as he placed his money on *rouge* or *noir*, *pair* or *impair*, or when one of the people clustering around the green baize table smelt too strongly of scent (women could often be found there) or when some Pole and his wife persisted in bobbing up and down in front of him, preventing him from seeing the red numbers which he wanted to bet on, and forcing him to place his money on the black, thereupon, of course, losing – and sometimes he would take Anna Grigor'yevna with him, but then she would distract him and he would lose because of her and get angry with her with the result that she soon decided that she had brought him bad luck and stopped coming, although he kept on demanding that she should do so and got angry with her for refusing.

She started to take walks around Baden-Baden and its environs, avoiding the smartly dressed Russian ladies – but all the same, one day she decided to walk down the Lichtenthaler Allee, setting off down the Lichtenthaler Strasse in order to do so, but found herself for some reason in the wrong place – at a Catholic monastery – and she entered the courtyard, wandered around it for a while and then turned back home – and on one occasion she set off on a long walk and after a couple of miles or so climbed up some steps and found herself in the Altes Schloss, where a tea-garden stood in one of the courtyards – Anna Grigor'yevna thought all this exceptionally beautiful, but she was a little worried at having walked quite so far, being afraid of slipping and falling over and thereby losing the future Sonechka or Misha – and besides, Fedya was probably already sitting on a bench in the avenue beneath the old chestnut-tree – she could tell without fail from a long way off by his simple appearance if he had lost or not – his black hat would be lying next to him on the bench, his face would be pale, his hands placed on his knees as if he were about to get to his feet, his face looking anxiously around, staring at the figures of people appearing in the distance in the depths of the avenue – and she sometimes found it extremely comical that he would not notice her walking right up to the bench, and still searched for her somewhere in the distance, occasionally tearing one hand away from his knee to use a handkerchief to mop away the beads of sweat appearing on his temples and forehead, that deep, receding hairline above the sincipital lobes so carefully and, on occasion, so exaggeratedly reproduced by painters and especially by sculptors – and he would be looking straight at her but, for some reason, through her and he would carry on peering into the far distance of the avenue while she already stood beside him, almost laughing – *almost*, because he might be insulted – 'I lost the lot,' he would say, hurriedly rising from the bench at the same time as she sat down to get her breath back and cool herself with her fan – 'And where have you been?' he would ask suspiciously, looking her up and down from head to toe as if she were a stranger – and a few minutes later they would already be walking home along the neatly paved streets, lined with neatly clipped trees, past neat German houses with their shutters closed to keep out the midday sun – and he would be walking slightly ahead, holding his black hat which he had bought in Berlin at the insistence of Anna Grigor'yevna and which looked more like a bowler, but now it was too hot to wear it, and besides, it reminded him of the hat depicted in a so-called friendly cartoon but, in fact, a caricature, printed in one of the issues of *Illustrated Miscellany* soon after his story 'Mr Prokharchin' had appeared in Krayevsky's *Notes of the Fatherland* – the cartoon showing him bowing and scraping in front of Krayevsky and holding exactly the same kind of hat in his hand – or rather, no, I think that he was still wearing the hat and was only *about* to take it off – and the hat was drawn disproportionately large, like his head, so that his trunk and his foreshortened legs formed a kind of appendage to his head and hat, doubtless intended as an allusion to his exaggerated idea of his own intellectual capacities and talents – and a few years later, when his period of hard labour was over and he was in exile (and even *that* didn't stop Panayev, that buffoon with his drooping and eternally damp-looking moustache, and his ilk), there appeared in *The Contemporary*, in a comic, even taunting style, a note to the effect that he, Dostoyevsky, was asking Nekrasov to print *Poor Folk* with a gold surround – but the most terrible thing, however, was that, in an argument with one of Panayev's supporters, in the heat of the moment when he was nearly passing out with rage, he had actually shouted out something to the effect that, in comparison with the rubbish that was getting printed nowadays, they certainly *should* print his works with a golden surround to show the reader the difference between a *real* literary work and tawdry twaddle and that it wouldn't hurt some writers and critics to realize this, either – he had been alluding to that suave Turgenev who had once listened to his ideas with an expression of cheerful amazement and even of innocent surprise, as if it was the first time he had ever come across so original an opinion – and that sincere expression of sympathy seemed to egg him on further and further – and he was desperate to astonish that rather naive gentleman even more, to captivate him with his ideas and at the same time to warm himself with the pride of his own dreams – and on and on he went, ever deeper into himself, revealing all, because in his mind's eye he could already see himself soaring somewhere high above with Turgenev, his bosom friend and someone he so admired, and could see the glory of that young but already famous writer becoming his glory, and his own prestige, Dostoyevsky's – that of a writer just setting out but already well-known in his turn – reflecting on Turgenev, and the two of them, each lighting up the other with his glory, exchanging it, bathing in its mutual rays, would rise above everyone else who would be enraptured by so unusual a friendship, so extraordinary, so unheard-of an infusion of hearts – and then Turgenev suddenly began to trip him up, so innocently at first that you might have thought it accidental, unintentional or even by mistake – but gradually it became clearer to Dostoyevsky that he had simply blundered into a carefully constructed labyrinth or an invisible snare and he was helplessly flailing about within it, trying to get free – and he suddenly saw himself seated on a chair in front of that high-and-mighty gentleman, squirming about, trying to rise to his feet, his hands on his knees for support, but with his body refusing to obey him – and he continued to sit there, his face reddening and then draining of colour, and all around people laughed at him and his friendship! – and Turgenev, his idol, casually resting his elbow on the back of the chair and placing his coldly gleaming lorgnette to his eyes, also laughed with the rest, as he gently stroked his well-groomed beard – and the words he had uttered during his argument with one of Panayev's supporters were also meant to apply to Nekrasov and Belinsky, who for some reason at a literary soirée had both sat down to play preference (such a dull pastime!) at a card-table somewhere to the side near an alcove, ignoring Dostoyevsky as if he did not exist – and he purposely went up to them several times during the evening, peering at their cards, realizing full well himself that it was becoming embarrassing, and although he gave a little cough from time to time, they did not even look up: it was as if he did not exist at all – and once, having been invited to Belinsky's house, he thrust himself upon his host and Nekrasov as a partner, but as soon as he sat down, they got to their feet and withdrew to the other end of the drawing-room, where a lively conversation had begun about Princess Volkonskaya's latest lover and a small circle had formed – and he continued to sit, pressing his palms together until his bones clicked and his fingers began to hurt – could that really have been the same Nekrasov who had appeared at his apartment in the early hours of the morning (it had been during the white nights, so it was light outside), who had appeared at his apartment puffing and panting as if he had run the whole way from his own flat to Grafsky Lane where Dostoyevsky lived, who had appeared at his apartment, holding the manuscript of *White Nights* behind his back, as if it were a present? – and could that really have been the same Belinsky who, having read the manuscript, received him at some unearthly hour in the study of this same house, sitting his guest down opposite him next to an enormous desk heaped high with papers and trying to maintain a pedagogic tone of voice but failing, and then jumping up from the desk and beginning to walk rapidly around the study, talking excitedly and waving his arms about, all this passion and enthusiasm fermenting into pure exultation being directed at him, Dostoyevsky, and his novel – and an hour later he stood on Nevsky beside the house where Belinsky lived, at the corner by the Fontanka River, looking at the deep-blue sky, the passers-by, the careering carriages, and everything that had taken place seemed unreal because he had not even dared to *dream* that it could happen to him – and a few days later the whole of literary Petersburg – and even non-literary Petersburg – began to talk about him – Belinsky introduced him to all his friends like some celebrity, serving him up as you might serve some piquant dish at the end of a banquet – and he caught fleeting glimpses of the distinguished grey heads of Petersburg personalities with side-whiskers and decorations in their button-holes bowing reverently towards him, and the eyes of women he dared not even dream about gazed at him with interest, coquettishly, flatteringly, and the hum of conversation in drawing-rooms would die down whenever he entered – and could this really have been the same Belinsky and Nekrasov who had now so indifferently got up from the card-table as he had sat down, trying to foist himself upon them as a partner just to remind them of his existence, hoping that by his presence, by his interruption, he could wrest from them a few complimentary words about *The Double*, at the very least some reference to it, it did not even have to be complimentary, let it be critical, anything but this cold silence! – and how absorbed they seemed to be now in their discussion at the other end of the drawing-room surrounded by the latest talentless mediocrities fashionable in the salons of Petersburg, how interested they seemed to be in that society gossip about Princess Volkonskaya, those so-called progressive minds, those men of letters!

He sat by himself at the card-table, bending his head lower and lower and pressing his chest against the hard edge of the table, so that it became difficult for him to breathe and every beat of his heart thundered in his ears, drowning out the lively murmur of voices which now floated from the centre of the drawing-room where the whole circle had drifted – and he pressed the palms of his hands even tighter together between his knees, and, despite the candles burning brightly in the crystal chandeliers, the faces of all the people present at the soirée looked grey to him – then he got to his feet, but instead of walking to the entrance-hall, nonchalantly throwing on his overcoat and leaving this house on Nevsky Prospect, beside which – not so very long ago – he had stood not daring to believe in the realization of his dream – but instead of this, like a tiny fish, attracted by invisible chemical substances to the jaws of some marine monster, he headed towards this circle, pushing his way through the guests and looking avidly into the eyes of Belinsky and Nekrasov who had, of course, already become the focus and centre of attention, and he attempted to make some feeble witticism, begging to be noticed – and he began to argue with someone, shouting excitedly, at the same time knowing that he uttered absurdities – and then, abandoning all hope, he began to agree with everything said, but nobody listened – and the giant sea-monster swam on, not even deigning to swallow the tiny fish, ignoring such a small and unappetizing object.

The dwarfish midday shadow thrown by his bent and slightly stooping figure was following him to one side, gliding over the grey cobbles of the roadway – a stunted shadow because the sun was high, almost at its zenith, and it was the height of summer, so it was surprising anyway that a man's shape and the trees and the houses should be casting any shadow at all – Anna Grigor'yevna was walking with him, but slightly behind, her shadow gliding along after his, as short as the other, though more elegant somehow, despite the fact that the future Misha or Sonechka had altered her figure – and occasionally his shadow would superimpose itself on hers if he slowed his pace down slightly, or they started to walk a little faster – and sometimes the shadows would even cross, though it may just have been an illusion, as this was a contradiction of the simplest laws of physics.

Once or twice, here in Baden-Baden, he had bumped into Turgenev and Goncharov in passing – Goncharov used also to visit the Panayevs, but in those days they had not made each other's acquaintance – in fact not meeting until after his exile – Goncharov, just as sluggish and bloated a gentleman as his creation, Oblomov, used to receive 400 roubles per printer's sheet, whereas he, Dostoyevsky – for all his poverty – used to be paid only 100 – and the man's eyes looked putrefied somehow, like those of a boiled fish, and he exuded the smell of bureaucracy, although with his income he had no need to work, and it was probably through miserliness – not that this prevented him staying at the Hotel Europe, however, the best establishment in Baden-Baden – the place where Turgenev had stayed as well as Litvinov from *Smoke*, that bloodless hero of a bloodless novel which also contained the venomous windbag Potugin, working hard to revile Russia while bowing low before the humblest German burgher – Potugin who visited Litvinov in this very hotel, so exclusive that Anna Grigor'yevna and himself would not even have been admitted to the lobby, as they were so poorly dressed – and at this same hotel Litvinov was secretly visited by Madame Rotmirova, the beautiful Irina, the general's wife, who, lowering her veil, would walk silently in, and at other times Litvinov would make his way just as secretly to her room in another fashionable hotel with carpeted staircases where he and Anna Grigor'yevna would also not have gained admittance – and all this accompanied by Potugin's orations declaiming that Russia should long ago have sunk down into Tartarus and that, if it should indeed happen, nobody would even notice.

He had seen Turgenev for the first time not very far from the Kurhaus, promenading down the avenue with some lady or other, his large head bent slightly forward, now and again nonchalantly fingering his lorgnette on its golden chain as he listened – and people out for a walk slowed down as they pass-ed by and then turned to have another look at the famous writer – and Dostoyevsky also slowed his pace, mechanically somehow, without even realizing it, and then suddenly he felt the urge to dart off sideways, but it was already too late – Turgenev had noticed him, his features feigning an air of joyful astonishment, as if the encounter with Dostoyevsky was an extremely pleasant surprise for him, as if he had never expected to see *him* – with *his* ideas – amid the overdressed throng roaming idly around this European spa-town, al-though Turgenev knew perfectly well that he *was* there – his gambling was a secret to nobody – and Turgenev was dressed in a light-weight grey suit, and his companion was also decked out in something fashionable and expensive.

'Fancy meeting you here, old fellow!' he said in that high falsetto of his, so out of keeping with his imposing figure –

and stopping for a moment, he raised his light, white hat a little, revealing the whole of that celebrated lion's mane, now beginning to go white and for that very reason, as his admirers, and particularly his female admirers, used to maintain, particularly noble.

'*Permettez-moi de vous présenter Monsieur, er...,*' he said, hesitating for a moment, as if he were searching for the name, '*Monsieur Dostoyevsky,* a former engineer and now a man of letters in Petersburg' – and a slender hand in a dainty glove was carelessly proffered in his direction – and when he went to take the hand and make some genteel remark, about the weather, I think, or possibly something else, the hand, fragrant with some special daytime perfume, was no longer there, and Turgenev and his companion were already lost to sight – and he was still standing there in the same place, wearing his black, out-of-season suit and with a black hat in his hands, like Trusotsky in *The Eternal Husband*.

Turgenev never lost the opportunity of calling him an engineer or, in the last resort, a *former* engineer, emphasizing the apparent artificiality of Dostoyevsky's involvement with the literary world where he, Turgenev, was rightful king and Dostoyevsky was nothing but an upstart, a parvenu – and they had met again a number of times after his return from exile and had even, as it seemed, become friends once more, taking part in one or two charitable functions together and exchanging letters as Dostoyevsky attempted to enlist the services of Turgenev in his journal *Time*, which he edited together with his brother, several of which he sent to Turgenev abroad, asking him to dispatch the story 'Phantoms' for the journal as quickly as possible, but it somehow turned out not to be *asking* but *begging* and in a frenzied kind of way – and in the same letter he wrote that he wanted to see him and that their last meeting had left some unexplained matters between them and that they should meet again in order to sort things out – and all this he wrote several times in the same letter, but once again it came out in a frenzied kind of way, as if he were trying to thrust his friendship upon him and, because he realized that, he became even worse – after the resumption of their friendship Turgenev had at first treated him with a certain care, perhaps feeling sorry for him, but then this solicitude began to give way to the old feigned amazement inviting the other to reveal everything, and although the traps and snares were not as evident as they had been in the Panayev period, he had to be on his guard the whole time and even so occasionally stumbled, feeling like a tightrope-walker who could slip at any moment and hurtle down below – and the rope along which he crept felt less and less steady every time, and on occasion he could scarcely keep his balance, only managing it by holding his arms outstretched to both sides – and those eyes, full of spurious interest and feigned sympathy, egged him on to perform all his 'steps' – faster and faster – until he slipped and fell into the abyss – and just to hear that false laughter, to try and earn the least bit of reciprocal candour, he would have been willing to dance the cancan, even if he had already slipped and was hurtling downwards, pirouetting in the air as he did so.

Placing the coldly gleaming lorgnette to his eyes, Turgenev watched him with condescending grace, as he sat opposite in his spacious hotel room with its white, gold-inlaid furniture, its ornamental ceiling and its enormous windows, draped in crimson velvet, the visitor having succeeded in avoiding the manager who had unceremoniously barred his way the day before, announcing that the gentleman was not at home – but this time, however, walking past the glass door to the hotel as if by chance, he had chosen a moment when the manager had left the foyer to go somewhere, and quickly went in through the door – and from there, without looking round, as if someone might shoot him in the back, he practically *ran* up the carpeted marble staircase and onward, as if he were being chased by a pack of hounds – and then he slowed down a little, trying to recover the necessary dignity as he proceeded down the corridor, passing a large number of white doors with golden monograms.

'Ah! It's you!' said Turgenev in his woman's falsetto, greeting his guest with that ingenuous smile of his, full of joy and amazement, clad in a long dressing-gown which made him look even taller than he was, with his dark, copious, slightly greying beard, his celebrated mane of hair and an interested, inviting expression in those dark-grey eyes of his, slightly flecked with green.

'I have heard so much about you *and* your novel, although I haven't yet had the good fortune to read it myself,' he said, escorting the guest into his spacious study containing a large desk strewn with books and manuscripts and a copious couch, covered with a carelessly folded plaid blanket and some cushions.

'Now, let me have a proper look at you,' said Turgenev, moving back a few steps from his guest, like a painter appraising his picture, and he raised the lorgnette to his eyes for a moment. 'Well, you really do look like a genuine writer now, especially with that shirt-front!' – and the greenish sparks smouldering in the depths of his eyes flashed briefly into life and then faded again, his face resuming its earlier expression of pleasure and interest – 'But do make yourself comfortable,' he said, moving a hard chair towards his guest while settling himself in an armchair, placing one leg over the other, the long, narrow slipper, decorated in the same way as his Turkish dressing-gown, shaking slightly.

He and Anna Grigor'yevna had chosen that shirt-front in Dresden where it had caught his eye because it seemed quite unusual, the corners of the collar being slightly rounded, and they had decided that it was very fashionable – and yesterday Anna Grigor'yevna had spent a long time ironing the thing – so there he was, sitting down, looking uneasily from side to side, not knowing where to place his hat – and had he really come here to listen to all this? – was that why he had humiliated himself in front of the hotel manager so as to sit here feeling like some wretched dropper-in or, to be more accurate, beggar, although he wasn't begging for anything? – and at any moment he would probably begin to dance his cancan, standing as he was on the edge of a precipice – only one step more and he would slip and go hurtling into the abyss – and he still sat looking around himself helplessly.

'I am sorry about the slight mess,' said Turgenev, catching his eye, 'or, as the Germans say: *Unordnung.*'

'Well, in my opinion, you became a German a long time ago, so you've nothing to be sorry for,' he blurted out somewhat illogically, as always happened when he wanted to throw out a barbed remark, but only making himself more angry – and the step over the edge of the precipice was taken – 'And your novel is German through and through . . .' – and now he hurtled down and there could be no returning – and Turgenev's face gave a strange wince as he leant back in the armchair and put the lorgnette in front of his eyes like a shield – but his visitor, placing his hat on the white and gold-inlaid card-table standing between them, thrust forward with his whole body, like a fencer removing his sword from its scabbard.

'I take your words to be praise,' replied Turgenev, parrying the blow – 'A literature which has given us Goethe and Schiller . . .' – and his guest made another lunge forward: 'You have never known or understood Russia, and as for Potugin, that pitiful seminarist of yours . . .' – 'And, of course, Russia seems to use such extremely effective means for instilling obdurate patriotism,' returned Turgenev, referring, of course, to penal servitude, and hitting below the belt – 'So why don't you go to Paris and buy a telescope so you can examine Russia from there,' he blurted out in one breath, having read somewhere recently about some telescope set up in Paris.

Turgenev sat back in his armchair once again, hiding his eyes with his lorgnette-shield – and they fought with swords, as they sat there on either side of that round, inlaid card-table, inflicting pin-pricks on each other – and this duel has gone down in the history of Russian literature as the quarrel between Dostoyevsky and Turgenev based on ideological disagreements concerning the relations between Russia and the West.

Slightly more than a hundred years later arguments between Slavophiles and Westernizers, which had been extinguished apparently for ever by the coming to power of the workers and peasants, have resumed with renewed energy – through the man with the hard and penetrating gaze and two melancholy creases furrowing his forehead, conveyed under escort to the airport at Frankfurt-on-Main, a city whose streets the Dostoyevskys wandered up and down en route to Baden-Baden – this man who arrived in a foreign country as an eternal visitor and settled beyond the ocean in one of America's northern states, whose landscape so distantly reminded him of the snows and forests of his native land and made those relinquished realms seem much more beautiful to him than they were or could have been in reality – this man who picked up, as a runner takes the baton in a relay-race, the hilt of the sword used in battle more than a century before by Turgenev's visitor and now, swinging it bitterly around, began to hack at the air, annihilating to left and right – and he stood on a high mound of snow next to the parcel of land containing his country house, surrounded by barbed wire – standing there hatless for some reason, as if he were in a graveyard, and the wind blew his smooth, straight hair, grey by now and thinning, and his beard, also grey, was covered with hoar-frost and icicles hung down from it – and it did only seem to be the air he hacked at, for his fellow-countrymen would be peacefully sleeping or watching an international hockey match on television, supporting their home team and fortifying their patriotism with the appropriate beverages, shouting: 'Get in there, Sasha! Slay the buggers!', slapping the obdurately angry or exulting palms of their hands against their own or their neighbours' knees, and then going drunkenly on to watch the evening news, which would show, amongst other things, film of a piece of traitorous scum, as the newsreader called him, standing on a mound of snow, and waving a sword – and digging a neighbour with an elbow, they would shout: 'Oi, Kolya! Why didn't they shoot the bastard, eh?' – and every morning, after swigging a mugful of kiosk beer, they would buy their beloved copies of *The Star* or *Komsomol Pravda* and, without hurrying, would tenderly smooth them out on their knees on the bus or tram as they travelled to work at their building-site or factory, eager to discuss the highs and lows of yesterday's hockey and, during their lunch break, or perhaps without even bothering to wait, have another drink – and the man who had taken the sword from Dostoyevsky's hands hacked bitterly at the air, accusing the West of not understanding Russia and the paths of its future development which should be founded entirely on its national spirit – and he, together with those who shared his thoughts, crossed swords with those who held a different view of Russia and her future, including one particularly prominent man with thinning grey hair, unassuming grey eyes and gentle features, his uncertain expression more than made up for by the determined face of his wife, a dark-haired, dark-eyed woman with a stubborn chin and confident bearing – and *she* was the one who had placed the sword in his hand, and when it slipped, *she* was the one who would give it back to him and would close her hand round his so that the sword would not slip again, guiding his hand, as though teaching a child to write – and the two of them stood on the rampart of an ancient Russian city where they had been compelled to live, with the golden cupolas and the whitewashed walls of recently-restored church-towers and cathedrals with their apses and arched gables shining behind them, but their gaze was turned towards the West – and the man standing on the mound of snow on the other side of the earth looked towards the East, towards his homeland – one of history's paradoxes which turns out to be no paradox at all, but a predetermined plan.

The man and woman standing on the rampart in fact held on to a flag-staff rather than a sword, and the giant white sail-cloth drooping down to the very ground rippled in the wind, revealing in turn various inscriptions, now black, now red, now yellow, exhorting, cautioning or commanding people – and there they stood, arms thrust forward and upward, gripping the flag-staff, vaguely resembling the sculptured figures in front of the entrance to the Exhibition of Economic Achievements in Moscow symbolizing the dictatorship of the proletariat and the peasantry (as well as productions of the 'Mosfilm' studio!) – the bronze worker with bulging muscles, like an anatomy textbook illustration, and the collective-farm woman in her kerchief, both stretching their hands forward and upward together to grasp the mighty hammer and sickle – and someone's invisible but formidable and relentless hands were attempting to drag down from the rampart the man with uncertain features and

56

his dark, determined wife, but they carried on waving their flag with its inscriptions, the different colours appearing in turn, like an illuminated sign – and the man's arm was pale with swollen veins in the elbow, as his heart-beat was irregular and he had to be given frequent injections – and his fellow-countrymen hated him even more than the one who had now entrenched himself on the other side of the world, and regarded him as a Jew – and before his enforced exile to the ancient Russian city he travelled the entire country, making demands, forcing his way through police cordons, urged on by his wife who helped him unfurl, in the most improbable places and at the most unexpected moments, that enormous white flag with its constantly changing instructions, collecting around him small groups of incomprehensible, suspicious-sounding foreigners festooned with film and cine-cameras which probably contained photographs of all the locks on the Moscow–Volga Canal as well as of all the Moscow railway termini and the queues for oranges or meat which they would later use for military purposes or the spread of make-believe reports about our country – 'Hands off!' our fellow-countrymen wanted to shout as they stood in their queues or killed time beside ticket-offices waiting for them to open – but they did not know if they were allowed to, because no instructions had been issued, so they said nothing, and this hostile, resentful silence of theirs was declared by the man who waved his flag and broke through the cordons, to be the silence of slaves, and a score or so of others cried out the same thing – and they also waved flags, only smaller ones, and they also appeared unexpectedly in the most improbable places to unfurl these pathetic little pennants and gather their little collection of foreigners, in order to pass on state secrets and sell their motherland – and no doubt they all have long hair and long noses, so let them go to their own country and wave their flags about there with that leader of theirs, whose wife has that foreign-sounding name, and who is tarred with the same brush anyway – exile the lot of them, to the back of beyond, or better still: shoot the buggers, the whole long-nosed, worthless lot, and do away with the rest of their crew at the same time, and then that fellow holed out on the other side of the world will see he's going to all this bother, waving his sword around, to no purpose – that his country has been developing in the necessary direction without his help and advice – on the basis of its national spirit.

The shadows of the two Dostoyevskys glided over the cobblestones and were lengthening as they approached their apartment, because it had been a fair walk from the avenue of chestnuts where Fedya had sat on a bench waiting for Anna Grigor'yevna – and the sun roasted his back through the black frock-coat which he had bought in Berlin.

The morning after he had visited the hotel, when they were just on the point of drinking their tea, Marie brought them a thick, glossy visiting-card announcing in flawless copperplate all too familiar a surname – the early hour having been chosen by Turgenev on purpose, of course, as a polite insult – whoever calls on people at *that* time? – and was it for this he had danced the cancan at his hotel? – and for a moment he pictured Turgenev's face to himself with its characteristic expression of feigned astonishment – no! – the face had not worn its customary expression that last time! – Turgenev's eyes had followed him through the lorgnette extremely intently, as if the lorgnette's owner were afraid he would be bitten by a mad dog at any moment – and this thought pleased him so much he even smiled – and in their rooms it was cool and dark, even peaceful, the workmen in the smithy probably being at their lunch, and the children having spent all night and morning emitting piercing shrieks, now asleep – and he wanted to take off his heavy frock-coat briefly and lie down for a while, but Anna Grigor'yevna had opened the windows and shutters, which she was always so careful to lock whenever they went out, being afraid of burglars, fire and thunderstorms, and together with the fragrance of acacia blossom and bright sun, sounds from the street entered the room – the clattering of horses' hooves on the cobblestones, the occasional loud remark exchanged by women in the courtyard, the rumbling of carts delivering water or beer – no, he could not permit himself to do that now – he *had* to go – and Anna

Grigor'yevna, compelled by his imperative look, took her bag with a sigh and extracted a few gold coins from it which he stuffed with a trembling hand into his waistcoat pocket, although he did have a purse – it was quicker that way, and much more convenient for him when gambling, as he could bet more easily when he did not know how much he had left, undistracted by thoughts of how much remained and the game undisturbed by having to engage in unnecessary calculations.

He walked with his body bent slightly forward, his shadow gliding along behind him as the sun was now shining from the front – and he would ply between their lodgings and the Kurhaus several times a day, deviating from his route only to look in at the post-office (but money from the publisher Katkov never arrived), or a shop, or the market to buy fruit and flowers for Anna Grigor'yevna on his way back from the casino, whenever he had won – and in general, he would be on an upward climb, despite the smell of perfume wafting from some of the ladies, chance visitors staking one coin at a time, and also despite Jews and Poles who would block his view – on an upward climb, even if he sometimes stumbled or, against all expectation, began suddenly to fall, thinking each time that it was all over, but it would turn out to be only a foothill on the route to the summit which would slowly but surely draw closer, sometimes even visible through breaks in the cloud, covered in virgin snow, gleaming silver in the rays of the sun or even reflecting gold – and for the others – Turgenev, Goncharov, Panayev, Nekrasov – they all remained below at the foot of the mountain, hand in hand in some kind of round-dance, enveloped in the fetid mists of the lowlands, prancing about, full of empty vanity, and craning their necks to look enviously up at him as he climbed towards the unattainable peak, unconscious of the all-consuming sense of liberation which he felt, just as they were ignorant of the passion which compelled him to go on – he *had* to, he was obliged to cross the threshold.

As he approached the casino, he began to take smaller steps so that the number of paces from their lodgings should add up to exactly 1457 as, according to earlier calculations, that number was his most successful, and it always led to his winning – not that there was anything strange about that, the last figure being a seven and all the figures together adding up to seventeen (yet another seven) – and there was something special about seven, an unremittingly odd number, divisible by nothing except itself and one, and this was true of it not only in its pure form, but as a unit of two-figure numbers as well – 17, 37, 47, 67 etc. – it was a very special number – and now he had almost reached the bottom of the steps leading into the building and had to make his steps really tiny – almost mincing steps, managing all the same to make them finally add up to his figure of 1457!

He walked across the broad entrance-hall with its fountain surrounded by a few Frenchmen engaged in animated conversation, and up the wide staircase with its tasteless classical statues to the first floor, ready to begin, as always, with the middle, and largest, hall, his heart pounding as if he were about to have an assignation – and, feeling his waistcoat to make sure that he had not lost any of the money, he pushed his way through the crowd of curious onlookers around the table and announced he was placing three gold coins on *impair*, because three was an odd number – and now he was calm – the main thing having been to push his way through this crowd of alien and hostile people, to push his way through without anyone insulting him, or without it *appearing* that anyone had insulted him, and no less important had been the need to begin the game, in other words, to declare himself – and whenever he tried to shout out his stake and position, it seemed that the eyes of all those sitting or standing at the table were turned towards him and that they all believed he was gambling for the money, out of necessity, and so he always tried to announce his bet as clearly and carelessly as possible, but always managed to sound either too pleading or too defiant, so that people must still be thinking that some extremely special, pressing reasons were compelling him to gamble – and now all this was behind him – and he went on to win, and on the seven as well – double luck and a good omen – and, having won three gold pieces, he now placed all six on *impair* – and won again though on the nine this time – he must switch to *manque* as *passe* had already come up three times in a row – and he staked five of the nine gold coins he had won – he was winning time after time – on *passe, manque, rouge, noir* and even twice on zero – the coins were piling up before him – and someone obligingly placed a chair behind him, but he did not sit down in case he altered the tempo of his game and, in any case, he was probably quite unaware of the chair and what he was supposed to do with it – and everything around him spun in a kind of mad vortex – nothing was visible except the piles of coins before him and the tiny ball, rolling round and finishing in the sector he had divined – and he was betting over and over again, raking in with his hands the coins he had won and adding them to the pile which shone with a reddish-gold gleam – and the peak of the mountain had suddenly emerged from the clouds, which remained somewhere below – he was now so high he could not even see the earth – all was covered with white cloud, and he strode across the cloud and, strangely, it supported him and even lifted him up towards the reddish-gold, unconquered peak which until quite recently had seemed unattainable.

'You have taken my coin, sir!' someone's ugly, rasping voice rapped out – 'Please be so good as to return it!' – the crowd of players and curious onlookers standing around the table was still circling about him, like people riding on a merry-go-round – and someone began to tug at his sleeve – a gentleman with a squashed, clean-shaven face and a dyed moustache who stared at him intently with bulging, colour-less eyes, saying something in French, but with an unpleasant accent, either Polish or German – and the merry-go-round suddenly came to a halt, although all the people riding on it remained at a rakish angle through inertia – frozen as in a tableau vivant, but with their eyes fixed on him, and even the croupiers, seated at either side of the table, raised their impassive faces – and he suddenly realized that he was being addressed and that somehow or other he had managed to rake in a coin belonging to this unknown gentleman, but what significance did this hold compared to his flight up towards the peak which had revealed itself to him? – and he mumbled some excuse and said that it was absent-mindedness, as he continued on his way, through inertia, floating in the clouds, unaware of anything else that was going on.

'I don't think it was absent-mindedness at all!' snapped the stranger in his rasping voice, staring at him as defiantly as before and breathing the smell of steak and red wine into his face.

For a moment he thought he had seen all this a long time before, and with extraordinary ease he tumbled headlong downhill to where some familiar figures began to emerge from within the marshy mist, still performing their strange round-dance, which no longer seemed so contemptible – and hand in hand, they sang some verses and in between the couplets shouted out some words, and these words concerned him, but he could not make out their meaning, although, taking everything into consideration, the words must be ridiculing him – and others took part in the dance as well – but he could not make out their faces yet, although one did seem to be becoming clearer – a purple face with lynx eyes, and there were women's faces, too – and were they not the ones which had peered through the barred window to the guardroom? – and, muttering incomprehensibly again, he tried, I think, to hand the stranger a coin, but he had already gone – and all he could see was the stranger's receding back somewhere in the distance, well beyond the circle of players and onlookers surrounding the table – '*Podléts*', he muttered, 'Scoundrel', probably because that is the kind of thing people say in such circumstances, but he said the word in Russian, softly and indistinctly, as if addressing himself – and, hands clasped behind his back, the stranger withdrew in triumph, evenly measuring out his every step like the departing Commendatore.*

A strange silence had fallen on the gaming-hall, although the business was over – and the yellow light from the crystal chandelier forced its way with difficulty through the tobacco smoke, and the corners of the hall were lost in gloom – and

---

* A reference to the threatening figure who brings retribution on the hero in Mozart's 'Don Giovanni' and Pushkin's 'The Stone Guest' (Translators' Note).

suddenly it seemed as if he had just pulled some cotton-wool out of his ears, and he could hear voices speaking, someone coughing – people proved to be moving and talking, the croupiers yelling the results, the gamblers shouting their stakes and positions – so he played on *passe* and won, but already this resembled the flight of someone mortally wounded – and the next bet was lost – and then he staked on zero, immediately reducing his pile of coins by nearly half – and the fall continued – Turgenev's face, expanding now to disproportionate size, expressed both feigned amazement and sympathy, and his large figure stood out from the others engaged in the round-dance, accompanying it with little comic refrains, while the others continued wildly dancing and singing.

The daylight took him by surprise when he emerged onto the street as he thought night had fallen long before – but husbands were coming back from church or from a walk, their wives at their side and holding their children by the hand – carriages and coaches passed by on the road, and then a black cat ran in front of him and, through habit and superstition, he stopped before he realized that it was a little lap-dog and, also, that nothing else could happen any worse than the event which had just taken place – 'Canaille!' he snapped and struck the stranger's face with the back of his hand, hitting that barrel-head with its squashed, protruding ears so hard that it made his arm ache – the stranger tottered and began to sink slowly to the ground – the gamblers and onlookers parted to make room for him on the floor and then gathered around him, while others rushed towards his assailant to escort him from the room – but with breathless frenzy he sent them all flying and, returning to the gaming-table, succeeded in breaking the bank on zero – and there he was at the very peak of the mountain and, as far as the eye could see, stretched infinite space with toy cities and dark-green forests looking, from that height, like low bushy thickets and, beyond them, the boundless, blue sea merging with a sky of equal blueness – and even better would have been slapping his face with a glove and continuing to play, calmly placing his stakes as if nothing had happened, or perhaps challenging him to a duel – there they were, early one morning, somewhere on the outskirts of Baden-Baden, in the ravine beyond the Altes Schloss, approaching each other from a distance of twenty paces – and he aimed at the stranger's chest, but at the very last moment, before shooting him, he magnanimously forgave him, and the stranger fell down on his knees before him and kissed his feet, and he raised him from the ground . . .

A man wearing a dark suit and no hat, because he had left it behind in the cloakroom, walked along the Lichtenthaler Allee, waving his arms about and occasionally muttering, oblivious of the people about him – and the warm summer wind from the Schwarzwald, the Thüringer Wald, or wherever, blew his thin hair about, which made the bumps above his temples look even more prominent.

The train stood at the platform in Bologoye, the second and final stop of this non-sleeper on its journey from Moscow to Leningrad, the doors in between carriages banging as some young lads and soldiers, letting in clouds of icy steam, jumped down from the train without overcoats on and ran along the snow-covered platform to the one open kiosk which was illuminated by a paraffin-lamp and selling locally made pies and bottles of beer, the colour of concentrated urine and foaming slightly at the top.

During the journey the carriage-windows had become glazed with a thick covering either of ice or snow, but through this greyish-white crust, as though through closed eye-lids, you could make out the station-lights and the shadows of people running – and somewhere to the north-west, a hundred or so kilometres away, beneath a double shroud of night and ice, lay Lake Il'men' with its three apexes, or even more because, as is usual with lakes, some river or other flowed in at every conceivable corner – Lake Il'men' with ancient Novgorod spread over the hill at its northern shore, Novgorod with its bell-towers and churches dating back to the tenth or eleventh centuries, built in a solid, austere manner with tall, narrow windows like embrasures, and golden cupolas crowned with eight-cornered, lattice-work crosses symbolizing Orthodoxy.

Reflected upon the light-blue surface of the lake were gentle white clouds, and drifting slowly across it was a paddle-steamer, wheels cudgelling the water and splashing the deck where the Dostoyevskys stood together with their two children admiring the beautiful summer morning – and as he looked at the receding cupolas of the Novgorod cathedrals, Fyodor Mikhaylovich bowed in their direction and crossed himself with three fingers, so fervently as to leave dents in his coat which now seemed to hang off his shoulders which had grown thinner of late – and almost immediately Anna Grigor'yevna, in her black travelling shawl, also bowed and neatly crossed herself, and then the two of them made the sign of the cross over their children, Lyubochka and Feden'ka, their most precious little children, as they invariably called them in their letters, because Sonechka, whom Anna Grigor'yevna had been carrying in her womb in Baden-Baden, had died soon after her birth in Geneva.

The steamer, bearing the name 'Hero' which was painted in elaborate gold script on the semi-circular casings covering the wheels, crossed Lake Il'men' and reached the southern shore, entering the mouth of the little river Lovat' and beginning to travel slowly upstream, first along the Lovat', then along the Polist' which flowed into it and finally along the Pererytitsa, following the meandering river-courses, carefully avoiding sandbanks, hooting out warnings to barges coming in the opposite direction – and then the bell-towers and churches of Staraya Russa appeared in the distance, and the Dostoyevskys bowed and crossed themselves several times again and made the sign of the cross over the children.

On Cathedral Square, not far from the Church of the Resurrection, stood the house where Grushen'ka Men'shova* lived, she of the delicately curving little toe and the sweet voice, who had been abandoned by her lieutenant fiancé and was a great intimate of Anna Grigor'yevna, confiding in her the affairs of her heart to such an extent that Fyodor

---

* Grushen'ka Men'shova was the 'real life' prototype of Grushen'ka Svetlova, the heroine of Dostoyevsky's novel, *The Brothers Karamazov* (Author's Note).

Mikhaylovich was even occasionally jealous – the same Grushen'ka who in the novel had been disgraced by an officer in her early youth and was then taken under the wing of a rich and debauched merchant – and it was this very house which Dmitry Karamazov had left on the night of the terrible murder when he had gone by way of backyards and kitchen-gardens to visit his father, Fyodor Pavlovich – this house stood at the apex of two streets and had a large garden and bath-house surrounded by a high fence, where the Dostoyevskys lived when they came here from Petersburg every summer and occasionally in the winter – and in the deserted alleyway at the back of the house, overgrown with thistles and nettles, Dostoyevsky discovered a butterfly larva under one thistle or, rather, a cocoon with a mysterious kernel, emitting a sickly-sweet odour of incipient decay – and it is possible that he may even have taken his trophy home with him – and the rooms in this house were partitioned off into little compartments, creating numerous nooks and crannies, mezzanine floors, staircases and all kinds of secret places – and under the same thistles Fyodor Pavlovich Karamazov had found Stinking Lizaveta wearing nothing but a hempen shirt – was there not something exquisitely humiliating about the fact that Dostoyevsky had given him his own name, Fyodor? – and the partitioned rooms of old Karamazov with some staircase or other leading upwards, witnessed a battle between father and son over Grushen'ka with Alyosha, Ivan and Grigory the servant trying to restrain first Dmitry and then Fyodor Pavlovich who kept on crying out: 'Grab him! Grab him!' as Dmitry managed to break loose from the grip of his brothers, overthrowing partitions, furniture and some vases as he hurled himself towards his father, knocking him to the ground with a terrible kick and beginning to smash his head in with his foot.

'Now, that's what I call a *real* beating!' I heard someone say behind me – and tearing my eyes away from the screen, I turned around and saw them, sitting there, taking it in turns to swig from a bottle, and this gulping noise continued until the end of the film – and from various corners of the auditorium, like the plopping of stagnant water, you could hear sniggers and cackles, especially during Ivan's conversation with the devil about faith and the immortality of the soul – and they guzzled beer and vodka like a group on that trade-union trip 'In Dostoyevsky's Footsteps through Staraya Russa', who would arrive at the place, dive into the River Pererytitsa and then, taking another swig, swim up to the ship's propeller and thrash about in the waves it created.

From his study in Staraya Russa he could see both Cathedral Square and the river embankment with the street adjoining it, because the house in which he lived was, as ever, in a corner position and the windows of the study were placed, furthermore, at the very apex of the house – and as he paced up and down the study, looking out of the window time and again at the cupola of the Cathedral of the Assumption, gleaming gold in the rays of the setting sun, he dictated 'The Grand Inquisitor' to Anna Grigor'yevna – and the fearsome judge in his black robes opened with a rattle of chains the iron door concealing the prisoner, dressed in raiment untouched after two thousand years and wearing a crown of thorns, as He returned to an earth just as sinful as in those distant times and experienced once again the same bitter taste of incomprehension and alienation and was condemned yet again to torment and suffering to redeem the sins of others (were they not also His own?), demanding of people such extremes of courage and suffering as only *He* was capable of – but the whole profound philosophical and religious essence of 'The Grand Inquisitor' was later expounded by Rozanov, declared by one contemporary to be spiritually in tune with the author of *The Brothers Karamazov* – and this harmony of spirit could possibly be seen in the strange knobbly cone-shape of his skull, or even perhaps in his strange and signal fate, becoming the husband of the woman who once travelled Italy with Dostoyevsky and shared the same cabin with him on board ship, where he pleaded for her friendship, and only friendship, and begged to be her confidant in that affair with the empty-headed Spaniard who passed himself off as a baron or viscount and then abandoned her like some dispensable object, like some threadbare dress, trampling on her feelings and her pride, which somehow made her even more desirable – but he had every reason to think that she later repented all this and in any case, a year before their ill-fated journey, while he was still in Petersburg, had she not visited him at his flat in the corner house by the canal, in the early autumn twilight, all shivery from the rain and the penetrating cold, with lowered veil, the natural heroine of many a Balzac novel? – or was this all his later imagining, or perhaps the invention of his biographers, or perhaps even her own?

The train had long since resumed its journey, leaving Bologoye far behind with its one spectral kiosk lit by a paraffin-lamp – and the carriage lurching from side to side together with all the passengers sitting in it, the frosted-glass lamp-shades and the suitcases, were all reflected over and over again in the dark windows beyond which the invisible snowy wastes drifted past – and I had to hold on to Anna Grigor'yevna's *Diary* to prevent it falling off the folding-table in front of me onto the floor and also to stop the words jumping about before my eyes.

When he arrived home, Fedya fell onto his knees before Anna Grigor'yevna so that she was quite taken aback and began to retreat into the corner of the room, as he crawled after her, still on his knees, and saying over and over again: 'Forgive me, forgive me!' and 'You're my angel!' – but she continued to side-step, so he jumped to his feet and began to drum his fists against the wall – and then he began to hammer his own head, as if by design, as though he was playing out some kind of farce, so that she briefly felt like laughing, but she was afraid that their landlady might hear and, apart from that, it might lead to another fit – so she ran up to him and tried to restrain him – and his face was pale, his lips trembled and his beard was twisted to one side – and kneeling before her yet again, he repented his losses and the fact that he made her unhappy, but she was unable to take in his words or understand the full depth of his suffering and humiliation and, standing in the corner of the room, she looked at him in amazement and even with an unfriendly kind of smile – could it be that she was laughing at him? – so he leapt up and began to drum the wall again so that, at last, she would have to realize, that they would all realize . . . Let the landlady know about it! Let them *all* know about it! . . . and he pounded the wall in a frenzy, but nobody could have been bothered because nobody stirred on the other side, and Anna Grigor'yevna continued to stand in the corner of the room – and he started to rush around, crashing into chairs and hurling them to one side, striking his head with his fists so hard that his hands began to ache – and she ran up and tried to restrain him, her face expressing nothing but fear now – So! she was afraid of the noise, of the publicity, nothing else! – and he pushed her away and started to rant on about jumping from the window that very second, knowing at the same time that he certainly would not.

They were both breathing heavily, as they looked at each other, she with fear and desperation, he with the hatred and hostility of a hunted animal – and his lips trembled as they had before, his face twisted by an agonizing convulsion – 'Fedya! Darling!' she cried as she rushed towards him and, cradling his head in her hands, pressed herself up against him – and all the injuries, afflictions and insults of the day which had built up inside him rushed to his throat in a sudden lump all at one go, as it used to be when he was a child, after the usual scene made by his father, when his mother would slip secretly into the nursery to see him and, making no sound with her feet, would go up to his bed and, thinking he was asleep, lean over him to stroke his face gently and kiss him – and the lump in his throat turned into sobbing, muffled and suppressed at first, but then increasingly loud, cathartic, agonizingly exquisite to the point of choking – and supporting him as she wiped his tears with her handkerchief, Anna Grigor'yevna led him to the bed, took off his frock-coat and waistcoat, helped him to lie down and covered him up – and it felt so odd that such a serious and clever man as her husband could cry – it must be a kind of fit, the same illness, and she was filled with a pang of pity for him and, at the same time, a vague feeling of responsibility, as if he were her child – and he still sobbed, but this was only water splashing against a boulder which has rolled down the bank into the lake – then she bustled about, wrapping his head in a damp towel, and he kept on kissing her hands and calling her his angel – and then, with many digressions and confusions, he told her the tale of the incident in the gaming-room, but she said that it was all right and that, *of course*, the stranger must have heard Fedya call him a scoundrel because everyone knew *that* Russian word, and if he hadn't understood, then all the others would have done so, and that he shouldn't have had anything to do with a scoundrel like that in any case – and he began to kiss her hands again because now he was doubly grateful to her, but after lunch, when they went for a walk down the Lichtenthaler Allee where many other people were out, Fedya started to collide with any man coming in the opposite direction whether alone or in the company of a lady – the squashed face and protruding ears of the gentleman who had insulted him, rose up before him again – and now he knew what he should have done: he should simply have pushed him, casually, but energetically enough for him to have fallen down or even just staggered or, failing that, for him at least to have realized he was not getting off scot-free with his wretched trick – and the stranger with the squashed face remained omnipresent, appearing one minute from a side-avenue with Fedya rushing to head him off, or walking behind him the next, with that measured, self-confident step of his, and he had to be diverted from that pace, a forcible intervention by someone else, or he would overtake Fedya and Anna Grigor'yevna and then have to be caught up with and given the requisite lesson – and Anna Grigor'yevna tried to restrain Fedya, but he kept on bumping into respectable Germans walking towards him or else he would suddenly try to overtake an unknown gentleman with the result that she would even find herself left briefly alone in the middle of this strolling, well-dressed crowd, gripping her parasol and lace shawl, the one given to her as a present by her mother and pawned by Fedya a few days later after yet another losing spell – but eventually she managed to entice him into one of the side-avenues where there were hardly any people, and from there they went to a concert.

A July evening was descending on the spa-town of Baden-Baden and in the distance violet storm-clouds hung over the Schwarzwald, the Thüringer Wald or wherever, and much further beyond there were flashes of lightning – and nearer the city, on the surrounding hills covered with dark vegetation, could be made out the Altes and Neues Schloss, red-brick with crenellated towers, as well as far more ancient courtly castles – and a few days later Anna Grigor'yevna was running up the stone steps of either the Altes or the Neues Schloss – escaping from Fedya who, after losing, was begging her for the last coin she had left, which she had to keep to pay their landlady because otherwise they would simply be evicted from the flat – and she ran up the steps with unusual ease, as if she were not carrying Sonechka or Misha at all, but then when she reached the third platform she suddenly felt ill with a terrible stomach-ache and nausea, so that she was obliged to sit down on a bench, and all the passers-by stared round at her, seeing that she was on the point of fainting – and when Fedya found her at last, he fell on his knees before her, there and then, on the platform in full view of everyone, as she buried her face in her hands so as not to be seen by strangers and because the nausea was rising into her throat – and he beat his fists against his chest, condemning himself for making her unhappy, but this did not scare her as it had done previously, because she had grown used to it – and she gave him the coin, although she knew that he would gamble it away, but in the meantime they sat in the meadow beside the Kurhaus and listened to an Austrian orchestra playing *Egmont*, and there was something in that music in harmony with the mountains towering in the distance and the violet storm-clouds hanging over them lit up by occasional flashes of lightning – and now the two of them clambered up a steep slope, she easily and quickly, following the capricious twists and turns of the path, which meandered through thickets, past high crags and the ruins of courtly castles, while he attacked the sheer and almost inaccessible rock face itself with its boulders and glaciers where no-one had yet set foot, slipping and falling and getting to his feet again, leaving, somewhere behind and beneath him, a sea of loudly laughing heads and dancing figures pointing up at him with their fingers – and occasionally the path she followed turned into a stair with stone or wooden steps, like the one which led to the Altes Schloss – and she ran up the steps, scarcely resting on the platforms, pausing only to look around at the majestic landscape which was opening out at her feet and then she would ascend the path again, twisting among the rocks and the alpine meadows filled with white flowers the names of which she did not know, while stones and large pieces of ice crashed down from beneath his feet, dislodging even more enormous rocks and ice-boulders as they did so, growing into a roaring, thundering mountain-avalanche which echoed and re-echoed its polyphonic reverberations through the foothills, drowning out the voices of the mocking crowd, that crowd of all too familiar faces, which continued to laugh, despite its dethronement, shouting out with dull, pig-headed incomprehension as it pointed up at him, with its enormous crude corporate finger smeared with dirt, bringing to mind the finger of one of the crowd in the painting of the 'Deriding of Christ' which he had seen in Dresden, though he could not remember the artist – Christ, wearing a crown of thorns which looked like barbed wire, sat on some steps, contemplative and detached, His elbow placed on His knee in such a way that His arm and long, slender hand hung lifelessly down, and one of the crowd, a strapping, coarse-looking fellow with sagging cheeks and a bulbous, red nose – a philistine's face – pointed a stubby, hairy finger at Him – and sticks and stones were being flung towards the man on the steps, and someone had spat in His face, already marked by physical violence, but still infused with profound thought and detachment – and the mob surrounding Him roared and laughed, and their laughter merged with the laughter of the crowd of familiar faces and was drowned out by the thundering echo and re-echo of falling rocks and ice-boulders, and he climbed higher and higher, overcoming the terrifying steepness, towards the very peak of the mountain, where, in a violet storm-cloud torn by flashes of lightning, lay the hidden Palace of Crystal, the dream of humanity, *his*

72

dream which he had cradled and nurtured deep within himself almost to the point of purposely mocking it – but now the avalanche drowning out the shouts and roars of those laughing faces, and the claps of thunder raining down from the violet cloud had inspired him with faith in the possibility of realizing that dream, and the vision of the painting by that unknown artist illuminated his path, and already he followed it, as he clambered up the steep face of the rock – and triumphant music – drums, horns, trumpets – poured down from the height where the orchestra played – and echoes of the avalanche occasionally reached Anna Grigor'yevna, but she continued as before along her free and easy way, following the well-trod path and ascending steps – and only in one place did her way cut across his – where the track followed a projection over the very rock-face where he struggled, as he clung to the fissures, slipping and falling, his clothes all torn, his arms scratched and bleeding – and she offered him her hand and helped him scramble up on to the path she was following, and now they walked on together, hand in hand – and although the melody being played by the French horns and flutes was still triumphant, you could already divine in it a kind of dragging, broken quality – and they sat side by side on the bench, listening to the music, he in his favourite pose, one leg crossed over the other, his arms hugging his knees, his eyes moist (or perhaps they had not yet dried from the tears), she sitting with her legs tucked a little behind her so as not to reveal her worn boots, feeling the cold and muffling herself in her shawl – and for a moment their eyes met and he took her hand and stroked it.

All around the little square with its central orchestra mound, benches were positioned for the public – and although it was still completely light, the lamps were lit, this double illumination giving rise to a wavering, somewhat spectral picture where things seemed either unfinished or not quite begun, and at night, when he came to her to say goodnight and they swam off, a counter-current began to force him sideways, and he felt he was drowning – she tried to help him, either by looking round at him, inviting him to follow her as she swam on ahead, or by swimming back quite close to him and staring straight into his eyes, holding out her arms and almost supporting him, or sometimes by plunging into the unknown depths of a green wave, trying to frighten him by disappearing – but he still continued to be dragged rapidly and inexorably away, scarcely struggling as the waves increasingly closed over him, the heaving green mass revealing those squashed features with the colourless, protruding eyes, the whole face swelling and inflating like a hot-air balloon, going crimson and turning into that all too familiar face with lynx eyes, and then arms belonging to scores, no, hundreds of those who the day before had been standing at the foot of the mountain, roaring with laughter and pointing in his direction, now stretched towards him, like the pincers of a gigantic scorpion – and although he made a few last despairing efforts, his body irresistibly wilted, and he sank rapidly and inexorably to the bottom.

And there he lay, his head settled feebly back into the pillow and his eyes closed, as she wiped the sweat from his brow, leaning on one elbow, and folds had formed where his head sank into the pillow, radiating out as in the painting by Kramskoy depicting him on his death-bed, but there was no trace of simplicity or tranquillity in his features now.

The violet storm-clouds over the Schwarzwald, the Thüringer Wald or wherever, having discharged all their electricity, turned into ordinary, grey clouds which headed slowly towards Baden-Baden, shedding drizzly rain on its sharp-ridged roofs and its cobbled streets – the summer was half over, and Anna Grigor'yevna, being glad of this respite, although many hot days still lay ahead, set about mending her dresses and underlinen, seated on the bed with her needlework, concealing as usual her feet in their worn shoes and hoping that the bad weather might speed their departure. Fedya as usual plied between house and casino, occasionally bringing home greengages, grapes and plums, moist from the rain, hiding them behind his back to surprise and startle Anna Grigor'yevna, but more often than not falling down on his knees before her, calling her an angel, begging her to forgive him for making her unhappy – and then she would tear herself away from her sewing and silently, suppressing a sigh, get up and go to the chest of drawers and give him her last friedrichs d'or, guilder or franc – and he hated her at those moments and became angry with her when she coughed or sneezed, because it was *her* money, her mother's money, and she meekly handed it over, without complaining, overwhelming him with her nobility – and again he would kneel before her, saying that he had stolen her money and that she ought to hate him, but he would always, in the end, hate her and himself even more – and she sneezed on purpose and coughed on purpose and sat at home like a seamstress, not wanting to go out with him – and what a pity it was raining, but then they still had umbrellas even so – and he put particular emphasis on the words 'even so', as if it was not his fault that they sat there without any money – but then, seeing the industry with which she was mending the holes in her dress (you could see the tip of her tongue as she worked), he was filled with a feeling of tenderness for her and pity and started to kiss her hands and the edge of her skirt as he knelt down again – and this time he really meant it with all his heart, and he gently stroked her shoulders and the back of her neck where her hair was pinned up, gathered together in a heavy knot, which made her look older somehow and, perhaps even, wiser – and even when she was not going out, she nearly always tied a scarf over her head, a sheer, diaphanous, black lace kerchief which made her look as if she was in mourning – and he would always ask her to take it off, which she did unwillingly – and kneeling by her side, he stroked her hair, burying his hands in it as her eyes looked at him in a heavy sort of way, glowering slightly, and he would call her his 'banshee', but she could not change her expression, even for him – and placing her needlework to one side and resting her chin on the palm of her hand, she gave a deep sigh and pensively began to stroke his head, as if she knew something which he did not and was trying to protect him from it.

He scarcely ever won now on either *pair* or *impair*, *passe* or *manque*, although he always managed to keep to the same 1457 steps, despite the rain and wind which hindered his walking – and entering the casino building, he would give his wet hat and umbrella to the doorman and then walk up the staircase – and as he went into the gaming-hall, heart beating, he would look around for the stranger, but the stranger would not be there and he would sigh in relief, because he was uncertain, if they were to meet, whether he could bring himself even to knock him with his shoulder – and the yellow light from the chandelier fell on the faces of the players and onlookers crowding around the table – and he tried to push his way through to the table and was seized for a moment by a feeling similar to the one he used to experience in his youth, as he sat down at a freshly laid table at Dominique's restaurant or Lerch's on Nevsky Prospect where he used to go in a riotous company – and he used to feel especially at ease and vibrant after the second glass of champagne as he thought of what lay ahead: the convivial toasts, the black caviare in tiny silver bowls, the laughter and possibly even a visit *there* – and with his tail-coat sitting on him very well, his freshly starched linen making his body feel pleasantly cool, and having the sense of being the centre of attention, the focus of everything, he would try to pronounce some particularly witty toast to subdue everyone completely – and on one occasion, when he was still working in the Engineers' Department, he and five or six other employees had decided for some reason or other to club together and drive to a restaurant – and a section-head was with them, his immediate superior, a rather dull-witted man with a large family and therefore always in need, completely under the thumb of his wife, who used to take all his money from him, down to the last kopeck – and he had happened to be present as they were making their plans to go, and expressed a desire to join in, not, however, contributing any money to the kitty, saying that he would give it to them later, not that anybody believed him, particularly as they knew from past experience that he would not cough anything up, taking him along most likely out of pure mischief.

That evening Fedya was in a particularly good frame of mind – the head waiter came precisely to him to take the company's order and, on the other side of the partition, you could hear the cheerful sound of voices and female laughter, and if you were to rise from the table a little, you could see the ladies' tall coiffures, their faces and even their bare shoulders – and the imbibed bottle of champagne gave him even more confidence, his mind already running with the witty toast intended to surprise everyone, when suddenly his boss, who until then had been sitting in silence, decided to make a toast himself – and rising to his feet, his face red with nervousness, he began to make some long and tedious speech about the benefit of government service to the motherland and other suchlike subjects – and people began to exchange glances and wink at each other – and when everybody had raised their glasses, Fedya, irritated that his own speech had been pre-empted, but inwardly still exhilarated, said: 'It's easy to make a toast if you're not paying for it!' throwing the words out, casually as it were, more to his neighbour than to anyone else, a limp, pale young man who worked with him under the same section-head – and he did not even attach any special significance to what he had said, until his neighbour whispered back: 'How can you dare say such a thing to *him*, for goodness sake?' – but Fedya, detecting no hint of reproach in his tone of voice, became only more convinced of his own wit which was obviously more brilliant than he had realized, others seizing his phrases in mid-flight so that tomorrow the whole department would be repeating his extraordinary witticism.

The next day the section-head summoned him into his office and began to reprimand him for some design which he had apparently executed incorrectly – and Fedya tried to prove to him that there was nothing wrong with the drawing, becoming very heated as he did so, while his boss remained seated, elbows planted on his large desk, his face flushed as if he had just drunk some more champagne, staring down stupidly at the drawing which lay in front of him – but when Fedya, who considered himself the victor in this argument, was on the point of leaving the room, the other man, without raising his head and becoming as red as if his face had been boiled, said to him: 'Wait a moment!' – his voice sounded strangled and quite hoarse – 'After you made that remark of yours, yesterday, I didn't know what to do. I should have slapped you in the face, but I didn't.'

Fedya stood in front of him, struck dumb with astonishment, feeling his heart begin to pound and the blood rush to his face and ears as if he *had* just been struck in the face – and the other still sat there, broad and squat, his head lowered like a bull with tiny, flashing, coal-black eyes, about to charge, and Fedya remembered that he had once told him that he had either Circassian or Georgian blood in him, from which he had inherited a fiery temper and a vindictive disposition, but nobody had believed this, thinking his only quality to be stupidity – and now, perhaps for the first time in his life, he had displayed his true nature – and for a moment Fedya even felt sorry for him, when he imagined the other's feelings the night before, and at the same time an involuntary respect for him and even a vague kind of fear – and he muttered some kind of apology as he did those few days ago at the Kurhaus during that business with the stranger.

'You're free now. You can go,' said his boss, and perhaps for the first time since he had started work in the department, Fedya was aware that this squat, obtuse and far from young individual was actually *his* superior, and from that moment on his life in the department became intolerable.

The first two, and sometimes even three, bets he usually won, and then the familiar merry-go-round of players and onlookers began to spin round him, and he was once again clambering up the precipitous slope towards the cherished summit with its Palace of Crystal, and somewhere down below the familiar figures performed their wretched round-dance – but then he began to lose, and the more he tried to keep to some kind of system, the more he lost – and then, abandoning any system, he lost again – and had to run home to get some more money for another try, almost immediately squandering it all again and having to run home for yet more money – and this resembled the medical condition known as obsessive-compulsive neurosis, when every attempt leads to even greater failure and at the same time an even more persistent impulse to repeat the attempt.

When the shortlived rains came to an end and the sharp-ridged red-brick buildings and dried-out, cobblestone streets began to roast once again in the merciless sun, the pattern of life led by the Dostoyevskys in Baden-Baden began to resemble a restless night when, even if you are sunk deep in sleep, you are still aware both of time passing and also of the endlessness of the night – so at first Fedya pawned his engagement ring, then the gold ear-rings and brooch belonging to Anna Grigor'yevna which he had given her on their wedding-day – and when he went off to pawn them, Anna Grigor'yevna, for perhaps the first time during this whole period, broke down and wept, wringing her hands, which was something she never allowed herself to do in Fedya's presence, or at least this is what she writes in her *Diary* – and having lost the money which he made from the brooch and ear-rings, he set out with her lace shawl, but nobody wanted to take it – firstly the jeweller, who told him that he only took gilt objects and mentioned somebody called Weissmann, but Weissmann's door was locked, and Fedya arrived home drenched through with sweat and rain because, despite the renewed sunny weather, there was the occasional brief downpour to refresh the streets and trees.

Then after lunch Fedya rushed off to Weissmann's again, but Weissmann told him that he did not deal in such things and gave him the address of a certain Mme Etienne, whose shop was situated on a square which Fedya could not seem to locate, although he had been there before, and for some reason he kept on finding himself in a side-street with a public baths – and at last he discovered the square, but after all this time the paper in which the shawl was wrapped had ripped because of the rain, and he was having to press the parcel firmly with his elbow to prevent the shawl protruding out – and there was no Mme Etienne in the shop, but another woman, emerging from the door leading to the rooms behind, told him that she was Mme Etienne's sister and that he should look in the following day.

So he rushed back home yet again, because he absolutely *had* to win that day, and once again he fell down on his knees before Anna Grigor'yevna and she gave him her engagement ring and he managed to pawn it with Weissmann, who, according to Anna Grigor'yevna, was a Jew and Fedya had had to wait around for *him*! – and on the money made from pawning Anna Grigor'yevna's ring, Fedya won one hundred and eighty francs, returning with the two rings which he had pawned, his own and Anna Grigor'yevna's, and a bouquet of flowers, but all this was simply the last breath of life before the final agony which was about to begin:-

Fedya rushed back and forth between home and the Kurhaus, dropping in at pawn-shops on the way or at the post-office in the expectation of receiving money from Krayevsky – and dressed in his black Berlin frock-coat and matching trousers, he would seem to be performing the most extraordinary movements, one moment turning into a juggler with black tights, white kid gloves and a black top-hat, skilfully throwing engagement rings up into space along with dresses and Anna Grigor'yevna's fur hat and just as skilfully catching them in mid-air, occasionally adding his own top-hat to this maelstrom of objects – and the next moment he would become a ballet-dancer, also in black tights and executing the complex steps of a divertissement against the background of Baden-Baden's red-brick houses, twisting on his own axis in pirouettes, stretching his arms up, first towards the sky and then towards Anna Grigor'yevna – and in response to his summons she would enter from somewhere off-stage, swathed like Carmen in the shawl, which he had not yet been able to pawn, and wearing a long skirt which concealed her worn shoes – and, as she appeared, he would stand on one knee and, clicking his fingers or a pair of castanets, perform a kind of serenade, while she tore off her necklaces and hurled them at him – and he would catch them in mid-flight and continue his serenade, deafening her with the sound of his castanets – then she would throw him her shawl and, clicking the worn-down heels of her shoes in time with her partner, would remove her dress and throw that over, too – and leaping up from his knee, he would fling necklaces, rings, dress and shawl into the air, juggling them skilfully, while she clasped her hands together at the back of her head, performing the gyrations of an oriental dancer –

but the objects he was throwing into the air did not return – and he threw up his top-hat, which disappeared as well – and then he took off his tights which turned out to be his Berlin suit and flung it somewhere up into space, too.

They were already four days late with the rent, and their landlady could well stop sending them lunch – and when Anna Grigor'yevna asked Marie for some boiling water in the morning, the maid replied that there was no point in burning wood for nothing – and was this really the same Marie, the loud-voiced young girl with the resonant *Jaa*, who had been ready to oblige to the point of inanity? – but then servants are always more honest than their masters, the glance of a secretary as you pass is an infallible guide to the regard in which you are held by her superior.

They were returning home down the Lichtenthaler Allee after their usual stroll, because nothing was left to them now but to go for walks or to pretend that they were – and Anna Grigor'yevna had no wish to go down this avenue in her everyday dress – almost the only one left after all the pawning – but Fedya insisted on having his way, and she felt that everyone was staring at her – and as the sun set, it lit up the mountain with the Altes and Neues Schloss – and Fedya stopped to admire the view and asked her to do likewise, to look at this picture, because it was an extremely rare moment when both castles and the mountain were all bathed in light at the same time – another minute and the castles would be sunk in shadow and this golden triangle would disappear – but Anna Grigor'yevna carried on as if the illuminated triangle, formed by the crenellated towers of the castles and the summit of the mountain, did not exist, carried on walking very fast, her body bent slightly forward if anything, and when he called out: 'Anya!' she went even quicker, almost breaking into a run – and he hurled himself after her, wanting to make her come back, if only for a few moments, before it was too late, before the angle of the sun's rays altered, but the moment had probably already passed: it had been lost, and because of her he had not been able to admire this unusual sight.

He ran down the avenue after her, breathing heavily and

bumping into passers-by – and she turned off into a side-avenue and for a moment disappeared from view, but then he caught sight of her figure, appearing fleetingly between the trees, and he thought that her face was covered by her hands, as if she was weeping – and they arrived home almost at the same time but still separately, she, entering the house panting and with her head lowered, afraid of meeting their landlady or Marie or even the other servant, Therese, he, running in, scarcely able to contain the rage that was choking him, and as soon as they were both in their rooms, he grabbed her by the hand and dragged her towards the door, but she broke free and threw herself on to the bed dressed just as she was, without taking off her shoes, burying her head in her hands – and why did she always spoil the rarest moments in his life? – would it really have been so difficult for her to stop, even for a moment, and look at the mountain bathed in light from the setting sun? – and he went up to the bed and tore her hands away from her face violently – but she was not crying at all – her eyes were closed and her face had a detached, almost stony look about it – ah! so she didn't even want to answer him! – and he started to shout – so she put her hands over her ears and began to shake her head from side to side, and then, scarcely opening her mouth, began to mumble incomprehensibly, as if to provoke him – and he rushed about between the window and the bed, now grabbing hold of her hands in an attempt to pull them away from her ears, now shouting that he would throw himself out of the window that very moment, but she took no notice and carried on mumbling, her eyes still closed as she shook her head from side to side – and then, flinging off his Berlin frock-coat, he tugged at his waistcoat so hard that the material made a tearing sound and the buttons were scattered all over the floor – and now pawning the suit without a waistcoat would be impossible, but that only made him even more irate, so that he now wanted to do something completely irreparable: to strangle her – and he knelt down next to the bed and began to peer at her face with hatred as she lay there on her back with her eyes closed, her lips pressed tightly together and her hands stuffed up against her ears, as if she wanted to cut herself off from the world around her – and then someone knocked at the door of the other room and, darting to his feet like someone caught red-handed, he ran through the next room to the door – it was Marie – perhaps she had been sent by the landlady, or perhaps she had come by herself, but as soon as she saw the lodger with dishevelled beard in his torn waistcoat, she opened her mouth wide and ran off like a shot.

When he came back, Anna Grigor'yevna was lying there with the bed-cover pulled right up over her head, and her worn pair of boots stood next to the bed, one of them toppling over on its side revealing a heel which was nearly half worn down: she had not been able to get them repaired after all – and then he was overwhelmed by a burning wave of tenderness and affection – and kneeling down by her bed once again, he began to kiss the edge of the quilt which covered her face, before lifting it a little, very carefully, to find that she was asleep, with a peaceful, gentle expression on her face, and the familiar sallowness, to do with her present condition, of course, showing on her forehead and even her cheeks.

The remainder of the evening he spent pacing up and down the rooms, after lighting the candle on his desk, occasionally going up to Anna Grigor'yevna to adjust the quilt – and perhaps he was pondering his article about Belinsky (which he never published, however), but most likely he was preoccupied with other problems, because the very next morning, with Anna Grigor'yevna's parting agreement, he crept out of the flat, carrying her lilac-coloured dress wrapped up in a bundle – and having successfully passed the landlady's door – because neither she, nor the servants, must see him with this bundle, of course – he walked out through the courtyard on to the street and, stooping a little with the bundle clutched tightly to himself, he hugged the walls of the buildings as closely as he could, like some gypsy horse-thief, running through the streets of imminently awakening Baden-Baden to Weissmann's and the five thalers which he received for Anna Grigor'yevna's dress he immediately staked on the first spin of the wheel and lost – and although this was something new, because he usually won on the first two or three spins, it did not surprise or even particularly upset him – and so he tumbled ever faster downhill, the speed of his irresistible fall taking his breath away, being struck by every obstacle in his way, without even noticing the knocks.

After leaving the Kurhaus, he rushed to the Hotel Europe, without being aware of any of the streets, oblivious of what he was doing – and his way was blocked by the thickset figure of the familiar manager who told him that Mr Turgenev had already gone away – but he did not believe him and tried to push past, aiming for the wide marble carpeted staircase, so that the manager was obliged to spread out his arms to stop him, as though he was driving a brood of chickens.

At that precise moment Goncharov appeared, walking unhurriedly down the stairs, supporting his heavy, swollen frame as he leaned on his silver-handled walking-stick and, catching sight of Dostoyevsky, he stopped on the bottom step of the staircase and lazily stretched out his pudgy hand from on high – sluggishly staring at him with those fish-eyes of his – and the manager withdrew unwillingly, like a guard-dog driven back into its kennel by its master – and Goncharov listened silently to his visitor who was telling him something in an impassioned way, waving his arms about and, puffing and panting as if he were climbing up the staircase again, Goncharov got out his purse, extracted three gold coins from it and gave them to his visitor – and then with a rapid bow, Goncharov's guest almost ran out of the lobby and rushed off to the casino building, losing all three gold coins immediately, almost with a kind of feverish willingness, as if he were possessed by an insatiable desire to lose, or were playing give-away draughts where the first to lose all his pieces wins – and the speed of his fall exhilarated him more and more – if he had been unable to cross a particular barrier in his movement towards the summit and was now hurtling downwards, then was there not also some kind of line or boundary *here* which would stop him? – because, after all, there were no external circumstances here, and all he had to do was surrender himself to this movement, to this physical principle, and so, shutting his eyes, he continued to fly downwards, the familiar figures performing their round-dance, now already somewhere above him, grinning and pointing their fingers at him again, winking and smirking meaningfully at each other – Turgenev with his majestic bearing, his lion's mane and his lorgnette directed towards him, Goncharov, wheezing after his six-course breakfast, Nekrasov and Belinsky, maundering on abstractly about some extraneous subject, Panayev with his pendulous, moist moustache and his drunken stare, and beyond them more figures and faces, familiar and unfamiliar, all exchanging glances and winks, pointing towards him – but, strangely enough, their dance seemed somehow pathetic – and they had not been privileged to experience the dizzy descent he had surrendered to – and the humiliating things were always median and mediocre, aiming at moderation and discretion – and this was precisely what *they* were – only an all-consuming, all encompassing *idea* could liberate a man, make him free and place him above everything else, even if the means of realizing this idea had to be a crime – and all these worthy gentlemen were incapable not only of surrendering themselves to such an idea, but even of beginning to comprehend it, and they were all constantly engaged in calculation and circumspection, subordinating their lives to material considerations.

He ran home and fell on his knees before Anna Grigor'-yevna, selflessly regretting the money he had lost, but not for one moment abandoning that exhilarating sensation of falling which made him feel superior to the surrounding world and even somewhat pitying towards his fellow men – and half an hour later he was already running along the scorching postmeridian streets of Baden-Baden, carrying in his hand a large bundle containing on this occasion his Berlin suit which Anna Grigor'yevna had mended while he had been away – and Weissmann was out, so he ran to Josel's, where Josel named a ludicrous sum, and he ran back to Weissmann's again.

Half an hour later he was pushing through the players and

onlookers, not caring about anything anymore and even *wanting* someone to knock into him or insult him, and he made his way through to the gaming-table – and of the twelve francs which he had received for the suit he immediately lost three – and that familiar breathtaking sensation of falling overcame him – let everyone see and know with what ease and even joy he was losing, the ones who trembled over every kreutzer, who calculated their every move – and he staked three more francs on *passe* and lost again, betting with extraordinary ease and just as easily pushing the money he had lost away from himself with the familiar merry-go-round turning about him, those figures with yellow, waxen faces like something from a cabinet of curiosities, hands in their waistcoat pockets, feeling around for some pitiful centimes or kreutzers, as they looked enviously at the ease with which he was losing his francs.

At this time there emerged from one of the side-avenues off the Lichtenthaler Allee with its well-dressed couples out for a stroll – Anna Grigor'yevna, walking determinedly along, almost at a run – and since early morning she had been doing a translation from the French, writing shorthand which only she could understand in a notebook epecially kept for this purpose, as she needed to prepare herself for earning their daily bread by herself, and she would sit at the lunch-table, the tip of her tongue industriously protruding between her lips, scribbling her little symbols and occasionally covering her ears with her hands, when the thundering of hammers from the smithy seemed to shake the table where she worked, but at this moment she needed to take urgent and decisive measures – and, after carefully examining the darn on the hem of her dress, donning her hat with the pinned-on flower and glancing at herself briefly in the little mirror, where she encountered a gloomy, glowering gaze which seemed to her very suitable for the enterprise which she had in mind, she slipped silently past the landlady's door – and as she approached the Kurhaus, she slowed down, trying to imbue herself with an air of confidence and nonchalance – and after ascending the stairs, she immediately made for one of the side-rooms, knowing that Fedya usually spent the first half of the day gambling in the main hall.

She took one franc out of her purse, which she had hidden there in case of dire emergency such as eviction from their flat, and spontaneously placed it on *rouge* – and won – and then she bet again – this time on *noir* – and won again – and she was overcome by the kind of sensation felt by someone who has hesitated on the edge of the water for a very long time and has finally taken the plunge to experience the entire delight of bathing – and she had already won ten francs, but this was not enough, so she began to stake more and more, and the little heap of francs which lay before her on the green baize began to diminish: she had started to lose – and standing next to her was a lady in a pale-coloured dress and a hat with a veil, also playing, but managing to place her stakes before Anna Grigor'yevna, because her veil kept catching on the flower in Anna Grigor'yevna's hat, preventing her from concentrating – but maybe Anna Grigor'yevna had learned this from Fédya who time and again would be hindered by someone as he placed his bet.

At this time Fedya, who was playing in the next room, unexpectedly won on *manque*, then on *rouge* and even on zero, and the more improvidently, the more wildly he bet, as if he still wanted to be the first player to lose all his pieces, the more likely it was that he won – and for one moment he even thought that this was the system: to play as he was, without any system, but this was only a passing thought – and the faces of the other players and onlookers started to circle around him again, although by now he scarcely noticed them – a *genuine* merry-go-round, revolving at mad speed so that the faces of everyone, gambling or looking on, merged together into a single yellow streak, but he could feel their jaws dropping with astonishment and envy, with *genuine* envy as they watched him win bet after bet, nonchalantly raking in the winnings – and how far away they were now as he climbed uphill once again, and the familiar faces performing their round-dance were already below him, and at the peak of the mountain, covered in cloud, the familiar Palace of Crystal peeped through – and he staked on zero and immediately lost nearly half of what he had won – and then on *rouge* and lost again – and around him everything suddenly seemed to grow dim – and triumphant looks, scarcely contained, were now visible on the faces surrounding him, while the merry-go-round now moved only by its own inertia – and once again he was flying downhill, bruising himself painfully against things and feeling that he had nothing to hold on to – and that whole theory of his about falling was worthless – he had simply invented it to make his injuries less painful, presenting the wounds to himself and everyone else surrounded by the self-sacrificial halo of some great 'idea' – but do we not all do the same thing, deceiving ourselves time and time again as we think up convenient theories designed to soften the blows continually rained on us by fate or to justify our own failures and weaknesses? – and is this not the explanation of the so-called crisis which Dostoyevsky went through during his penal servitude? – could his morbid pride ever have become reconciled with the humiliations to which he was subjected there? – no, he had only one way out: to consider these humiliations as his just desserts – 'I bear a cross, and I have deserved it,' he wrote in one of his letters – but in order to bring this about he had to represent all those earlier views of his, for which he had suffered, as erroneous and even criminal – and this he did, unconsciously, of course – the human psyche's need for self-preservation, especially the psyche of a man not too strong in spirit, incapable of slapping Krivtsov round the face, as one of the convicts had done, or of seeking revenge on those who insulted him, condemned him to this, not only against the dictates of reason, but radically altering any rational argument, adapting it to his own subconscious requirements, and only occasionally, at extreme moments in his life, like a voltaic arc in the submerged darkness, would those suppressed and saturated visions and images blaze up, illuminating with their merciless light scenes and tableaux from his life in penal servitude and exile, and then, shuddering, he would be forced to do mental battle with those who insulted him, being defeated even in this domain – and it was just such a spiritually redemptive feeling of guilt that he had experienced during the incident with the unknown gentleman at the roulette-table, and although this was not so much the case in his relations with Panayev and his supporters, here, too, he would occasionally try to ingratiate himself with Turgenev and would even get to the point of admiring him, all quite unintentionally and sincerely as he tried subconsciously to preserve his self-esteem and his pride, but despite the fact that the combat could take place in the intellectual and spiritual sphere, in *his* sphere, making the whole matter simpler, the visions and images of his trampled pride never left his side.

Outside the window which was covered by a dirty greyish crust of snow, the neon-sign 'Izhory Works' twisted by like a tiny glowing red snake – *Izhory* – practically Leningrad already, its outskirts, its dachas, its suburbs, inhabited by fairhaired Finns with their pale, passive faces – or at least that is what I preferred to think – 'As I was driving up to Izhory . . .' – I could not help remembering the line from Pushkin which for some reason always comes into my mind as I pass this spot, a tribute to conditioned thinking, as it is quite involuntary – and after this I invariably think of Pushkin eating Pozharsky cutlets, perhaps because of the similarity in sound between the words 'Izhory' and 'Pozharsky' or perhaps he really did use to eat Pozharsky cutlets there, as he awaited the team of post-horses, casually flirting with the postmaster's daughter – and along the highway leading to Petersburg, in the fading twilight, a blizzard would be raging, and the troika would be dashing away, sleigh-bells ringing, with the driver in his seat urging on the sprightly horses and the snow crunching beneath the runners – and sitting in the sleigh, wrapped up in a fur rug, would be Aleksandr Sergeyevich himself, hurtling towards Petersburg, pleasantly exhilarated by the wine he had consumed, by the beauty of the postmaster's daughter, by the anticipation of the balls he would attend in Petersburg and his imminent assignation with the next society beauty with whom he had begun a little affair on the eve of his departure – and forming by themselves in his mind were the verses which would later be reprinted from one edition of his works to another, and dozens of Pushkin scholars would analyse the rhythm and metre of these few lines and, arguing with each other to the point of anger and exhaustion at literary-critical seminars, attempt to establish the exact date on which they were composed, the motives which gave rise to them and the person to whom they were dedicated – Pushkin! – what a firm place he has found for himself in our hearts and minds – that swarthy, crinkle-headed little half-caste with the slightly protruding, light-blue eyes (disputes amongst experts about the colour of Pushkin's hair have not abated to this very day), then the mature Pushkin with his curly hair and not over-luxuriant side-whiskers covering the long, thin face, the whole effect being of slightly scrubby and none too tidy an appearance, and finally the Pushkin whose portrait hangs in the house on the Moika, with those pale, emaciated features and strands of hair sticking to his damp forehead, making him look like a hunted animal – and this is probably what he was like in the last months of his life and, perhaps, in the final days before the duel – that Pushkin who perished because of his cold, calculating wife who felt no shame at lacing up her corset in the presence of servants or even of the book-shop owner she had summoned to her boudoir in order to get another fifty gold roubles out of him for her husband's poems! – Pushkin! – a Don Juan, fervent and derisive, almost looking for a fight, who shot a pistol while naked in a hotel room in Kishinyov and then went strolling about the city dressed in a red nightcap, Pushkin, who grew the nail on his little finger like some foppish playboy or office-boy, Pushkin, who scarcely stood as high as the perfectly sculptured ear of his wife whom he nevertheless successfully impregnated on a yearly basis, still managing to be cruelly jealous of her, not always without justification – and if I were an artist, I would paint a picture entitled 'Pushkin's Marriage with Death', where I would depict Pushkin in a realistic manner, but Goncharova, his wife, with capriciously twisting lines, each one of which would symbolize a part of her body – arms, legs, head or torso – a really cunning ligature completely distorting our notion of the human body's proportions, having not so very long ago seen some similar pictures in the flat of a certain modernistic woman-painter obsessed with drawing female figures just like that, all extremely alike and apparently supposed to represent some demonic, if not satanic, principle, the lines symbolizing the arms and legs twisting and turning in many convolutions and just as stylized a body and head finishing as tentacles or simply joining together – and they could be followed only with the help of their creator, standing with a pointer in her hand like a geography teacher, demonstrating the direction of isotherms or isobars – but all the same it would have been in keeping for Goncharova, during their marriage ceremony, to twist one of these terrible lines round the neck of the real Pushkin – almost like Pushkin in the grip of an octopus – and all this may be extremely naive, of course, but after visiting that artist's flat I was often overwhelmed by the thought of such a painting and the next time I visited her studio I tried to suggest this theme to her, but she said that she did not exactly find Pushkin very exciting, the same applying to me by the way, and I was very pleased by her answer because I scarcely ever come across people who do not regard Pushkin as an idol – especially women, women poets in particular, from Marina Tsvetayeva who wrote of him as the 'terror of husbands, delight of wives', devoting an entire book to him and manifestly in love with him, to Bella Akhmadulina who celebrates him in that hazy, somnambulistic verse of hers – but you will probably never find as fierce and passionate an admirer of Pushkin as Dostoyevsky, for whom Pushkin may have been just as unattainable an antithetical dream as Stavrogin, embodying as he did harmony of spirit (though it may only have appeared that way), a high sense of honour (did Dostoyevsky know how loyally Pushkin used to bow to Count Orlov at the Mariinsky Theatre?), strength and constancy of character (did Dostoyevsky realize that the Decembrists did not really trust Pushkin very much, considering him both unstable and indiscreet?) and finally the nonchalance of a seducer who always achieved success (here there is really nothing to add in brackets, as Pushkin's perfection in this sphere was genuinely beyond dispute) – or perhaps the antithetical element lay elsewhere: Dostoyevsky the prose-writer was perhaps the most passionate poet and romantic of his age, while Pushkin the poet was possibly the most sober realist of his – but the most important thing, however, was that they lived in different times so that Dostoyevsky managed to avoid being the object of one of the poet's sarcastic epigrams – and if he had been, Pushkin would undoubtedly have been ranged with all the other literary enemies of Dostoyevsky and might even have held a leading position.

After losing nearly everything, Fedya with his few remaining francs headed out of the main gaming-hall into the side-room where, to his astonishment, he saw Anna Grigor'-yevna gambling, to begin with deciding that he must be mistaken, but no! it was her, dressed in her violet hat with the flower, and standing next to her were some unfamiliar men in tail-coats and a few ladies – and pushing his way through to the gaming-table he went up to her but she had obviously just laid her stake because her eyes were tensely fixed on the movement of the ball as it rolled rapidly round and round – and he took her hand – it was cold – and she started and, seeing him there, turned pale, but for some reason everything suddenly seemed extremely hilarious and droll – the phrase 'gambler-wife' came into his head and at the same time he was seized by a familiar feeling of tenderness and pity towards her – she had brought herself to do this in order – somehow or other – to straighten things out, to go back to the beginning – and taking her arm, he led her away from the table, her eyes filling with tears of shame and vexation, although she was looking at him as gloweringly as ever – 'Banshee!' he said, gently stroking her hand – and they left the Kurhaus and, in mutual silence, went down the side-avenue towards the mountains, she leaning on his arm and he looking time after time into her eyes, already dry from the tears and with a smile gleaming in them – and several times he repeated the phrase 'A gambler-wife, ai-ai!' as she began to see the humour of it herself . . .

They came out onto a hillside covered with bushes and began to make their way slowly uphill towards the Altes Schloss, Fedya being so cheerful by the time they reached the steps leading upwards that he started to dance about and stamp his feet in a particular way which he said was meant to straighten the worn and uneven heels of his shoes which needed to be made symmetrical – and as they headed off again, up towards the castle, he began to measure the number of paces between each bench along the way, lengthening his stride or shortening it to a mincing step as he approached each one – it was imperative that he limit himself to a particular number of paces, but it never seemed to work out and that was a bad omen – but Anna Grigor'yevna knew nothing of this and thought that he was simply fooling about.

When he had finished his antics with the benches, he suddenly struck a theatrical pose, getting down on one knee and beginning to wave an arm about, as if he were greeting someone – as he did this when he heard the sound of a carriage approaching, it was probably yet another superstitious gesture, but the carriage turned out to be empty with only one coachman sitting half asleep on the front seat – and Fedya and Anna Grigor'yevna laughed over this for a long time, before they began climbing up the narrow spiral steps to the highest platform of the castle, where Anna Grigor'-yevna was overcome with fatigue and sat down on a bench with a marvellous view opening out over the Rhine and Baden-Baden, while Fedya went over to the edge of the platform and cried out: 'Farewell, Anya, I am about to throw myself over!' – and somewhere far beneath them the blue Rhine meandered picturesquely and Baden-Baden spread out with its gothic churches, its sharp-ridged tiled roofs and its luxuriant green parks and gardens – and down there, to the left of the red-brick church, surrounded by greenery, was the white, almost toy-like building of the Kurhaus where, in the smoky air beneath the yellow light of chandeliers, money was being staked and lost with hands stretching out towards it, greedily raking it in – and all these gamblers were like marionettes from a puppet-theatre with some invisible person pulling invisible threads, and the puppets in their tailcoats with their yellow, waxen features jerking about, performing their unnatural movements – and how extraordinarily different all this was from the immense spaces revealing themselves as he gazed from the edge of the platform! – and swallows flew past almost at the same level as he was, and somewhere higher up, parallel to the crags overhanging the castle, some larger birds were hovering – mountain eagles, perhaps, or possibly hawks – and above even all this was the dark blue sky, so dark that it seemed almost to blend into some cosmic blackness giving the impression that stars would appear at any moment – and he felt a strange urge to fling himself from the platform where he stood and to soar off somewhere up and beyond, towards this blue-black sky, to merge with it, to merge with other worlds perhaps in the process of birth or newly-born and already inhabited by a human race experiencing its golden age.

Anna Grigor'yevna was now standing next to him, pale-faced, holding him tightly by the hand – and he led her back to the seat and, throwing himself on his knees before her, began to kiss her hands – how could he have forgotten about her and about Misha or Sonya, forcing her to climb up so high and frightening her with his ridiculous cries?

On the way back they called in at the post-office and asked for any letters – and there was one addressed to Anna Grigor'yevna, containing one hundred roubles sent to her by her brother Vanya – so now they could pay off the debt to their landlady, redeem the brooch, ear-rings, engagement rings and everything else and finally leave this accursed place – and they decided to do so the following day, so when they arrived home, Anna Grigor'yevna set about packing their suitcases, while Fedya went off to change the money needed to redeem the brooch, ear-rings and engagement rings – but, when the luggage was nearly ready, and Anna Grigor'yevna had decided to go out for a walk to meet Fedya, she suddenly realized that she had no chignon – she had been wearing it the day before and it was only today, going to the Kurhaus, that she had decided not to put it on – and it was probably that nasty Marie who had stolen it or purposely hidden it somewhere – it had happened once before – with her drawers – she had been searching for them

94

everywhere and then suddenly found them in the bottom drawer of the chest where Marie had almost certainly put them – and now that good-for-nothing Marie had hidden her chignon somewhere in revenge for not being given some pears once by Fedya and herself when they had given some to Therese – and now this was the second time it had happened – so she called Marie, but Marie said that she had seen the chignon the day before and that Anna Grigor'yevna had probably lost it somewhere, and then, when Anna Grigor'yevna asked her for the iron, Marie said that she was using it herself, and Anna Grigor'yevna had to bear this insult in silence.

It was precisely at this moment that Fedya arrived back looking pale and, after falling onto his knees as usual, he told her that he had gambled away the money which Anna Grigor'yevna had given him to redeem the brooch, ear-rings and engagement rings – and as she had to save the money that was left, Anna Grigor'yevna, with superhuman strength, lifted Fedya up off the floor and said that the two of them would now go to Weissmann's shop together, because she didn't trust him any more, and Fedya accepted this as his just desserts – and so they redeemed the suit, ear-rings, brooch and engagement rings and walked slowly back home, and the thought of the missing chignon never left Anna Grigor'yevna's mind.

When they arrived home, Fedya fell on his knees once again, begging for ten francs, only ten francs, to try his luck just once more, for the very, very last time, because he would never have another chance again – after all, they were leaving, and for this very last time he just *had* to win, if only a small amount, if only ten francs to equal the amount he was asking from Anna Grigor'yevna – but the main thing was to win without losing anything, not even a single franc, and then he would be able to leave with peace of mind because the last word would have been his, the last spin, and then all this would take on the appearance of an isosceles triangle which, despite having very acute angles and a blunt apex, at least would have some kind of peak – otherwise, it would all just resemble an ordinary horizontal line with nothing to crown it.

After receiving his ten francs and almost tripping on the slightly raised threshold of the door, he rushed down the stairs onto the street and then, panting with haste and excitement, ran onto the deserted Lichtenthaler Allee in the direction of the Kurhaus – and meanwhile Anna Grigor'yevna busied herself searching for the missing chignon and repacking one of the cases to make room for three plates, a cup and a saucer – and then Fedya came back, putting on a miserable expression but with a large packet of apricots hidden behind his back – and he had won first time and had then bet on *passe* and had won again, and had not bet any more – and that was an end to it – and so his eyes radiated such tranquillity and happiness that even to begin with he paid no attention to what Anna Grigor'yevna was telling him about the loss of her chignon, her suspicion of Marie and Marie's rude remark, but when he started trying to persuade Anna Grigor'yevna to eat some of the apricots, which he had carefully washed and laid out on a dish, and she refused them, beginning to search again for this ill-fated chignon, turning out the whole chest of drawers, he suddenly felt a surge of terrible irritation, not unlike the feeling of painful heartburn – of course, she *had* to spoil this happy moment in his life, this triumph, a petty, paltry one perhaps, but a triumph all the same, and just because of some wretched chignon he was now unable to savour the joy of existence to the full – and he had rushed specially to the other end of Baden-Baden to get those apricots, because all the shops had already closed, and he had only just been able to persuade the German, who was shutting up his shop, to sell them to him for his sick wife – '*für meine kranke Frau*', that was what he had said, wanting to move the German to pity, and humiliating himself in the process – and now she hadn't even asked him how he had managed to get hold of them so late, but had spent all her time searching for that damned chignon – so he started to shout at her that she was petty, that she always spoilt everything for him, and in any case, only old maids wore chignons – and she stopped her search, stood up straight and stared at him hard with that glowering expression – but not only were there no tears in her eyes, there was not even any reproach, only the defiance and cold despair of someone determined on a course of action – 'I am going away tomorrow by myself, first thing in the morning, and you can do what you like,' she said in a strange, unfamiliar voice and, walking over to the suitcases, she began to unpack his things – suit, underwear, handkerchiefs – placing them on his bed in such a way as to leave no doubt about her resolve – and he had never seen her like this before – she was a different person: he didn't know her – a young woman with a tired, almost haggard-looking face who in some incomprehensible way had appeared in the same room as him – no, he must have dreamt it all! – after all, this woman was supposed to become the mother of his children, of *their* children, and only today, a few hours earlier, she had come up to him as he stood on the edge of the castle and had taken his hand, firmly and tenderly, leading him away from the brink, as though he really had intended to hurl himself down below – and that meant that she must love him.

She carried on calmly repacking the suitcase and removing his things – and for a moment he imagined her actually leaving and himself left alone in these two rooms with the sparse rented furniture, the ear-splitting screams of the children coming from somewhere upstairs and the equally deafening thump of the blacksmith's hammer coming from the courtyard – and he imagined himself returning from somewhere to these empty rooms with nobody there to greet his arrival and nobody to rush and make him tea – and at night, if he were to wake up, he would go over to her bed to say goodnight to her, and he would feel her quilt and her bed, but the bed would be empty.

She carried on unpacking, and then walked over to the chest of drawers, without even bothering to look at him – 'Anya, you've gone mad!' he shouted, falling to his knees, crawling over to her, grabbing her hand and pressing it to his lips – and, still acting calmly, she removed her hand from his, and it was precisely this calm of hers which he found the most frightening thing – and he jumped to his feet, wanting to turn her face towards his, to look into her eyes, but suddenly the floor began to shake beneath him, and instead of her face, which he had expected to see, because he knew very well that he had taken her head in his hands to turn it towards himself – instead of her face, he saw some kind of strange, shifting, white blot, which began to expand rapidly, losing its whiteness and filling firstly with blue light but then darkening almost to the point of blackness, like the sky which he had observed that day, when he had been standing on the castle's edge – and yes, this really was a sky, nocturnal almost and filled with stars which for some reason were enormous, like the sun, each of them radiating a golden light, although it was perfectly possible to look at them, because they did not blind your eyes, and breaking away from the earth, he flew freely between them in space, but as soon as he neared one of them, the golden halo encircling the giant star would fade and his gaze would fall upon a stony desert area, so empty and endless it seemed to have no horizon, and scattered over the heaps of stone and the crags, which took on the hazy outlines of ruined cities, were human skulls and bones, and a strange unexpected smell emanated from these lifeless, stony wastelands – the smell of ozone usually experienced after a thunderstorm – and he flew on further and further, easily, effortlessly, like the birds he had seen earlier that day when he stood on the castle platform, but on all these stars, wherever he flew, he gazed at one and the same thing: the remains of earlier life, of former civilization – and everything was dead – and then the giant stars began suddenly to diminish in size and, against the background of the dark sky, a bright-yellow, full moon appeared, with a shield emerging from it on which were written in ancient ecclesiastical letters the words 'Yes, yes' – and this shining shield and the letters upon it moved across the entire sky from east to west, undoubtedly foreshadowing the messianic destiny of Russia, and he flew after the shield with such effortless ease that he lost all sensation of his own body, merging with what had earlier been inaccessible and had now become a part of his own flesh.

He was half-sitting on the rug between Anna Grigor'-yevna's bed and the wall, where she had dragged him, gasping under the weight of his body, and placed a pillow under his head – and his convulsions were already coming to an end, but there was foam on his lips, and so she wiped it away – and slowly opening his eyes, he looked at her without recognition – '*Comme ça*' he said in French for some reason – 'I'm here, Fedya, I'm here with you,' she replied, kneeling down next to him and pressing her cheek firmly to his cold forehead – 'I'm with you, I'm here,' she said again, and her words came out like a sigh of sorrow and tenderness.

The train from Baden-Baden was due to depart at two o'clock in the afternoon, but leaving without the chignon was impossible, and so the saga of the chignon-search began all over again early the next morning with a new vitality – first Marie being summoned, then Therese, to be subjected to cross-examination by Anna Grigor'yevna and Fedya, who, after his fit, was in a particularly bad mood, getting very irritable and even shouting – and when he had woken up in the morning, before even opening his eyes, he felt an unpleasant sensation and saw in his mind's eye a kind of triangle with an eroded apex – and exerting his mind, he had tried to recall what it was all supposed to mean, then suddenly remembered: the lost chignon – yes, it was precisely *that* making the triangle incomplete as they could not leave just as they were with the chignon still missing – and so Marie and Therese searched everywhere – and then Therese went away, and Marie began to look in Anna Grigor'yevna's bed, and then in Fedya's, and finally found it – down the side of Fedya's bed – and he started to insist that he had searched there himself earlier on and that the chignon hadn't been there, but as it had now turned up, Marie must have put it there herself – and with tears in her eyes Marie ran off to see the landlady who burst into the room and started shouting that her people were honest, that she didn't employ thieves, as she thumped her flat chest – this woman whom Anna Grigor'yevna used to call Madame Thenardier after a character in a novel by Victor Hugo, an inhuman lady with a loud laugh and masculine ways, but as she stood there now, shouting with rage and beating her chest with her fist, she reminded Fedya for some reason of another familiar character – 'Aha!' he thought: Katerina Ivanovna in *Crime and Punishment* at her husband's funeral feast, with red blotches suffusing her face and neck and consumptive breast heaving, frantically trying to prove her noble origins to the laughter of the assembled guests and more particularly to the contemptuous snorts of that obtuse and haughty German landlady of hers, Amalia Ivanovna – and how exactly he had managed to portray Katerina Ivanovna's type, although in this scene taking place now, the roles were exactly reversed – but how true to life the smouldering atmosphere was!

Since November of the previous year he had written nothing – first the wedding, then this roulette business had driven everything else out of his head so that he could not get seriously down to writing his article on Belinsky – but all these thoughts were only passing through his mind at random – and the landlady's voice could now be heard somewhere outside their door – the chignon affair was over – and he sat at his desk, resting his chin on his hands, eyes closed, and the familiar triangle with its eroded, jagged apex appeared in his mind's eye again – his winnings the day before had only been gained from two spins of the wheel – just one odd number, and especially the number three, could round things off – and it was still more than two hours until the departure of the train, time enough for him to win a whole fortune – and here he was, losing that final possibility, that last chance, sitting uselessly at his desk like this and at exactly the same moment over there, not very far away, at the end of the Lichtenthaler Allee in the white two-storeyed building with spires, behind the tall windows draped with heavy green curtains, on green, baize-covered tables, beneath the light of chandeliers penetrating the clouds of tobacco smoke – were the gleaming heaps of golden coins, like icon-frames in a church flickering in the candle-light, shrouded in clouds of incense.

After swearing to Anna Grigor'yevna that this would be the very last time, that all he wanted to do was to go and look, but asking her for just one guilder, just in case, he rushed off in the direction of the Kurhaus, while Anna Grigor'yevna, so as to pay less money for their luggage, began to wrap up all the books in her black dress and then put some into Fedya's overcoat as well, so that they could take the whole lot into the carriage with them as hand-luggage – and as well as this, she had to check all the drawers in the chest once again and the beds, too, so as to be absolutely certain that they had not forgotten anything – and by now Fedya was already back and on his knees before her, saying that he had lost everything and that he was a scoundrel, because he had pawned his engagement ring once again – so now they did not have enough money to leave at all, and they rushed to Moppert's, just round the corner, to pawn her ear-rings.

The piles of golden coins still shone with their mysterious ecclesiastical light and, with only an hour and a half left until the departure of the train, Fedya with five francs in his pocket rushed back to the Kurhaus – and earlier, when he had lost and pawned the ring, he had become too excited and placed his seventh bet (an odd number) on zero, relying on the lucky number 'seven', and had lost the lot, and the croupier took his money and placed it in the general pile which he then levelled with the palm of his hand, obliterating its peak – and now he simply wanted to have another look at the heap of coins always to be found next to croupier A, to look at them at the moment when they formed an apex.

Standing on tip-toe at the back of the players and onlookers, he tried to peer between heads to see the pile of coins next to the croupier, now decreasing, now increasing according to the progress of the game – and clutching the five-franc piece in his hand, his heart seemed to stop as he waited for the moment when the pile of coins would recapture its sharp, crowning apex – and he felt that that moment had to be decisive in his life, and when the heap of coins, which kept on growing as the croupier raked in yet more handfuls of lost money, when it grew so enormous that it looked as though it would collapse at any moment and something resembling a cone had formed on top of it, he, without being aware yet of what he was doing, thrust his way through to the table with one movement and, as soon as the croupier had invited people to place their bets, staked his five-franc piece – on an odd number once again – and the ball hurtled furiously about and almost immediately landed on zero, exclamations of joy and despair coming simultaneously from all sides, with some players scoring a huge coup and others probably losing whole fortunes.

He made his way out through the throng of Kurhaus visitors, his head sunk into his shoulders, his last coin gambled away, and with it his last hope – and he was hurtling downhill, finally and irrevocably now, and there above him, on the now forever inaccessible peak, standing in a semi-circle as though in an amphitheatre were the familiar figures with their all too familiar faces – winking at each other, smirking and chortling, pointing at him with their finger, and he was falling faster and faster, not even attempting to grab hold of anything.

When he arrived back home, breathless and pale, Anna Grigor'yevna was in the middle of an argument with the landlady who was demanding eleven guilders – and as she became heated, the landlady began to beat her breast again, shouting that at least she had a few more guilders than Anna Grigor'yevna and Fedya – and then she began to demand money for the service, money for the firewood – and Anna Grigor'yevna offered her two guilders, but the landlady said this was not enough, and when Anna Grigor'yevna added another guilder, she started to thump her chest again, shouting that there were no dishonest people in her service – and when she finally went away, Fedya rushed off to get a cab, but as soon as he had gone, she returned and began to demand eighteen kreutzers for a broken vase – and at this moment Fedya returned with a carriage, so soaked with sweat that Anna Grigor'yevna was afraid he might catch a chill, while the landlady kept running in and out of the room, demanding things and beating her breast – and at last, after hurriedly eating some bread and half a pound of ham that Fedya had bought when he went after the cab, they left their rooms and began to go downstairs – and the landlady did not come to see them off, and Marie, who was standing on the landing, did not even turn her head in their direction – what an ungrateful girl! – they had given her fruit and other small gifts so many times, and she didn't even want to wish them goodbye! – and the only people they met standing outside beside the waiting carriage were the blacksmith's nasty children, the ones who didn't allow them to sleep – and when they had climbed up into the carriage, the figures of the landlady and Marie appeared at the window, the landlady screaming some threat at them, and they fleetingly thought that stones might come flying towards them at any moment.

But the carriage moved off, the horses' hooves clattering over the cobble-stones, and they drove along the familiar Baden-Baden streets planted with white acacia trees, past the familiar houses with their tiled roofs and drawn shutters, through the hot afternoon (although summer was coming to an end), Fedya sitting all hunched up in his already worn, black, Berlin suit which he had redeemed from the pawnbroker's, and holding the bundle containing the books, Anna Grigor'yevna wearing her violet dress and the shawl which she had after all managed to redeem, and which now very usefully covered the patches on her dress – and she also had on her hat with the veil, and Fedya wore his dark hat which he kept on removing to wipe away the sweat, placing the bundle beneath his foot – and as she looked at the familiar buildings, and streets and at the chestnut-lined Lichtenthaler Allee which they were now driving down, it seemed to Anna Grigor'yevna that they had been living there a very long time, a whole eternity, and that, apart from this, there had perhaps been nothing else in their life, and she was afraid the whole time that something else would happen to prevent them leaving this place, continually looking up at the clock on the townhall tower which could be seen from different ends of the city.

Thank God! they had arrived just in time, and while the porter was taking their suitcases to the luggage-van, Fedya rushed off to get the tickets with the engine already getting up steam – and the bundle with the books which was destined for the compartment lay next to Anna Grigor'yevna on the bench, and at that moment Therese appeared, running down the platform, looking around from side to side – and Anna Grigor'yevna's stomach dropped – she had had a premonition that they would not leave the place, that something would happen to prevent it.

When she caught sight of Anna Grigor'yevna, Therese stopped and, out of breath, began to say something to her quickly – and it turned out that Anna Grigor'yevna had taken the key to the flat with her, so, breathing a sigh of relief, she began to rummage about in her handbag and found the key – taking apartment keys really was a bad habit of hers – and along with the key she gave a few kreutzers to Therese who thanked her and wished her a pleasant journey – and she was after all the best person in Baden-Baden, so obedient, so docile, and so embarrassed, of course, that they had been treated so badly.

The carriage was hot, but when the train finally got underway, it became a little cooler – and sailing past the windows were the red-brick buildings with their tiled roofs, and in the distance the green-covered mountains, one of them with the Altes and Neues Schloss and the rock-faces jutting over them – and now that they were leaving this place – never to return – she could see the beauty of it, as she had when they approached it for the first time, this city surrounded by mountains with the Rhine gleaming blue somewhere in the distance, and for a moment she felt sad – 'Parting, everywhere, is death,' wrote Marina Tsvetayeva, describing the feeling of sorrow which I, for example, experience when leaving even the most unpleasant habitation, probably because I know that I shall never return again.

Fedya had managed to get hold of some black grapes from somewhere, which were very tasty, and they ate them in the train, but, unfortunately, Fedya had not bought enough, and the familiar Schwarzwalds or Thüringer Walds stretched on and on outside, with people endlessly changing trains, one set of travelling-companions being replaced by another – two old women and a lady with an iron stick travelling to Basel, then an elderly lady with a stern face desiring, so Anna Grigor'yevna for some reason concluded, to get married, then a young German who trod on Anna

Grigor'yevna's foot, apologizing courteously – who turned out to be very loquacious which made Fedya immediately shrink into the corner of the seat and transfix Anna Grigor'yevna and the German with an angry look which boded nothing good – then a lady in mourning who was curious to discover whether there were still such things as passports in Russia and who took Anna Grigor'yevna for a German, which Anna Grigor'yevna regarded as an insult and even as out-and-out rudeness – and then two more young Germans – a newly married couple this time.

At one of the stations Fedya got off to buy some sandwiches, but it turned out that he did not have enough small coins, so he gave the vendor ten francs, receiving one franc short in his change – and Fedya told the man about this, but he pretended that he could not hear, busying himself with the other customers – and at this point the third bell rang, with Anna Grigor'yevna sitting in the carriage behind locked doors and the tickets with Fedya, who shrieked as loudly as he could that the man *had* to give him his franc back, to the extent of drowning out the whistle of the locomotive – and when Fedya burst into the compartment, dishevelled, red in the face and terribly agitated, he began to recount the whole incident to the loquacious German, adding at the same time very loudly that there were more thieves in Germany than everywhere else put together – and the two old ladies who were still in the carriage for some reason disagreed to each other just as loudly, but the young German concurred out of courtesy, so that Fedya obviously felt himself to some extent avenged for the sandwich disaster and for the German's rather obvious advances towards Anna Grigor'yevna – and outside the window the Rhine appeared once again, very wide with its water greenish and rocks in mid-stream, and Anna Grigor'yevna welcomed it as an old friend.

The next morning they arrived in Basel where a lot of people crowded at the railway station, and Anna Grigor'yevna and Fedya were quite unable to understand whether they were to wait for their luggage or not, but the loquacious German, who somehow turned up beside them once again, explained that their suitcases would be sent straight to Geneva – and so Anna Grigor'yevna and Fedya, who was carrying the bundle of books like Prince Myshkin when he turned up at Yepanchin's house, climbed into a tiny omnibus, Fedya treading on the feet of some English women, and then, after giving the bundle to Anna Grigor'yevna, rushing back into the station to enquire what would happen to their cases after all, and a few minutes later coming back to the carriage and treading on the English women's feet again.

The carriage rolled down the streets of this big city and then crossed a bridge over a wide river which Anna Grigor'yevna was pleasantly surprised to discover was the Rhine once again – and, standing by the railings on the bridge, were two or three old drunks, arguing about something and waving their arms around, leading Anna Grigor'yevna to ruminate on the illusory nature of freedom in Switzerland, after which the Dostoyevskys arrived at the hotel 'Zum goldenen Kopfe', where the waiter and the porters also turned out to be drunk, assuming Anna Grigor'yevna and Fedya to be part of the English family and trying to put them all up in the same room.

Having scarcely settled in, the Dostoyevskys went out to inspect the city, most importantly the cathedral and the local museum – and the day was gloomy so the pictures were badly lit, particularly in the cathedral although there was a little more light in the museum, but none of the pictures there particularly attracted their attention apart from one painted by Holbein the Younger and called by Anna Grigor'yevna for some reason 'The Death of Jesus Christ', although its real title was 'Christ in the Sepulchre' – and it had the form of an elongated triangle and, unlike the conventional interpretation representing the suffering or dead Christ with a touch of romanticism, it showed the corpse stretched out on a white sheet, as if in a mortuary, the nose elongated and the body tortured and lacerated and already marked by the first signs of decomposition, particularly clear on the face and on the disproportionately large feet, so that Anna Grigor'yevna viewed the picture in terror while Fedya was in ecstasy –

and noticing a chair standing beside the wall, he went over with rapid and decisive steps, placed it almost in the exact centre of the room, stepped onto it and fastened his eyes upon the painting – and the long picture extended horizontally right over the door in the Rogozhin house on Gorokhovaya Street – yes, and that was exactly how it should have hung, and Prince Myshkin, having seen this picture in Switzerland, would be uttering the precise thoughts of the man now standing on the chair, that 'such a painting was enough to make you lose your very faith', although the figure of the merchant with the tiny, fiery eyes, consumed with passion for that proud but fallen woman, had not yet manifested itself, nor that eternal heroine of Dostoyevsky's, morbidly arousing his feelings and for that reason unable to satisfy them, nor the actual figure of the Prince himself, that Knight of the Sad Countenance, half Christ, half Don Quixote, who suffered from the same disease as this person standing on the chair, nor the many other characters and personalities, nor the names with which he would endow them all, nor the events and scenes which would be played out, nor perhaps even the very slightest thought about his future novel, but for some reason this picture was a clear and complete detail – the first crystal to form in a supersaturated solution – and the remainder, perhaps still hidden by a thick mist, would have to come by itself.

He stared at the picture with renewed intensity – and for a few moments it faded, even seemed to dissolve, and in its place there appeared the familiar faces: the red one with the lynx eyes, the squashed one with the protruding eyes, and then the faces of those performing the round-dance, before positioning themselves in a semi-circle at the summit of the mountain, and beginning to point their fingers at him, sniggering and winking at each other, making him want to get down from the chair, but the next moment they all disappeared and he saw clearly once again the face and body of the dead Christ and heard the words about loss of faith spoken by someone else – and this idea was to become the focus of the novel, and then there began to emerge from the mist a few still indistinct objects, scenes and images: a gleaming knife – one peasant stabbing another and raising his eyes to the sky with the words: 'God, forgive me for the sake of Jesus Christ'; then a soldier selling his pewter cross, pretending it is a silver one; words about God uttered by a simple peasant woman as she sees her baby smile for the first time; an exchange of crosses between the two main characters of the novel; then an unusually deserted Summer Garden with storm clouds thickening over the Petersburg Side; a knife gleaming again somewhere in a dark corridor in one of the cheap Petersburg hotels near Liteiny Prospect and the quick glance of tiny, fiery, murderous eyes, and a knife gleaming again in the darkness as it is driven in beneath the white breast of the proud and fallen woman.

The attendant approached and pulled at the arm of the person standing on the chair – and Anna Grigor'yevna was standing next to him, apologizing for her husband's strange behaviour, afraid that they would be fined – and so he got down from the chair obediently, like a sleepwalker, not even noticing that he had been made to do so – and he walked beside Anna Grigor'yevna, first around the museum in order to find the exit, and then along the streets filled with carriages and omnibuses, past the large houses with their plate-glass windows, passing people hurrying somewhere, noticing nothing – and he was on the summit of a mountain, that very peak which had earlier seemed to be inaccessible, and from this peak there opened out a view over nearly the whole planet with its towns, rivers, little villages, oceans and churches, its entire life, bustling and full of tragic contradictions – and perhaps he was now in that same Palace of Crystal which he had stared at so fixedly as he tried to clamber up towards the summit.

They returned to the hotel 'Zum goldenen Kopfe' and had dinner, then went for another stroll around the city in the evening, and that night swam off far beyond the line of the horizon, their movements and breathing rhythmical, as they plunged into the water and thrust themselves out, and not once was he deflected by the counter-current.

Outside the snow-encrusted windows patches of hazy, dissolving light passed slowly by – lamps on the platform of

Leningrad's Moscow Station – and passengers stood impatiently in the aisle with suitcases and bags, the door on to the platform open and freezing steam billowing into the carriage – the train came to a halt – and, suitcase in hand, I stepped down onto the platform after the others and went among the bustling crowd of passengers and people meeting them towards the station building shining hazily through the frosty mist – and standing on the next platform was a van loaded with big blue sports-bags with hockey-sticks protruding from them – Moscow 'Dynamo' had been playing Leningrad 'Zenith' that day, and the team was now heading back to Moscow on the 'Red Arrow'.

The square in front of Moscow Station was almost deserted, the majority of passengers having disappeared into the Metro and the rest to the tram-stops to the left of the square, on Ligovsky Prospect in fact, or the Ligovka as it is known, and only a tiny handful of the bravest and most desperate were trying to catch one of the taxis which would drive up to the station from time to time – and around each car with its green light showing, a battle would take place – it was coming up to midnight – and in the light from the street-lamps and floodlights illuminating the square you could see the occasional, slowly descending snow-flake, while the frosty air made your nostrils stick together, and the snow crunched beneath your feet, and right in front of the square you could see the almost deserted Nevsky Prospect with its two rows of street-lights, gradually merging together and disappearing somewhere into the frosty, nocturnal gloom and with the occasional moving lights of the last trolleybuses.
 Walking around the square, I first of all crossed the Ligovka – and somewhere on the other side of the tram-stop, in the darkness sketched out by the dim line of street-lights, slightly to one side of the Ligovka itself, near the Kuznechny Market, was an ordinary, grey Petersburg dwelling-house where he had spent the last years of his life and where he had died on his leather couch beneath the photograph of the 'Sistine Madonna', given to him for his birthday by one of his friends, and this was where, driving in a taxi-cab into the

darkness somewhere, in the direction of that notorious district in the company of a painted woman, the hero of Bunin's story 'Noose Ears' had been heading, a story which for some reason literary critics consider to be the antithesis of *Crime and Punishment* – and then I crossed Nevsky at the point where it joins the square and came out on Vosstaniye Street, the former Znamenka – this was a street which he would often walk down on his way to visit Maykov, who lived there, or returning from the editorial or printing office on Nevsky back to Slivchansky's house, where he lived for some time himself, or to Strubinsky's house next to the Greek church, where he also stayed somewhat later.

On arriving in Leningrad I would always stop at the flat of a friend of ours who had lived on the Znamenka since before the war – and with snow crunching underfoot, the suitcase not weighing me down very much, I walked unhurriedly along, enjoying inhaling the frosty night air, looking at the lines of street-lamps, just as straight and even as on the Nevsky, merging together in just the same way and disappearing somewhere into the distance – and I stopped at a junction to allow a tram to squeak its way around the corner – two or even three carriages hitched up to each other with frost-covered windows through which you could just glimpse the solitary shadows of nocturnal passengers – and the house where our friend lived was right on the crossroads – I went in the familiar, dilapidated entrance where there was always a smell of cats and the stone floor was strewn with broken glass from bottles finished off by a 'troika' of drinkers or even a solitary one, and began climbing to the second floor up a steep, stone staircase with worn and broken steps, dimly lit by one or two electric lightbulbs – and outside the high door grown dark with age I turned the handle of the old-fashioned door-bell and, hearing no movement on the other side of the door, I twisted it again – Gil'da Yakovlevna had become rather hard of hearing lately – and at last I heard quiet footsteps behind the door and the sound of a bolt being pulled – and standing in the tall doorway, wearing a dressing-gown, was the tiny old lady, Gil'da Yakovlevna, with her wrinkled face, dimpled chin and dark hair which she had probably been dyeing for as long as I could remember and so had never been an old woman to me, only Gilya, as I used to call her as a child when we lived in the same city and when she was my mother's closest friend.

Bending down, I kissed her soft, wrinkled cheek and she immediately gave me a great smacker in return – 'Did you catch the train?' she began to say quickly – 'I thought the train must have been late. I was already ringing the railway station – What's the weather like in Moscow?' – and, bolting the door from inside, she ignored my replies and followed me into the room which I had already entered as if I owned the place – 'I've already made up your bed,' she said – 'Would you like me to heat up the pancakes for you, or would you like them cold? I've got some pies from Yeliseyev's shop, and is your mother still on her diet? Eat a bit of chicken – Anna Dmitriyevna cooked it. Tomorrow we'll have soup with dumplings, your favourite, and veal cutlets for the main course. I got them at the market yesterday. Do you use the market when in Moscow?' – the small round table was laid and covered with food, the old broken sofa was neatly made up and the snow-white pillow had another tiny cushion on it – 'Gilechka, why did you bother going to the market in a frost like this, and you could easily have waited for me to do something about the bed. Did you really *have* to lift up that incredibly heavy mattress yourself?' – but these reproaches were sham, as was the exaggeratedly sharp way in which she brushed them aside: 'Oh! do be quiet!', and both of us felt pleasant – this scene was repeated every time I arrived – and opening up my suitcase, I would extract a box of chocolates and some bananas, of which Gilya was very fond – 'You've gone mad!' she would say, not neglecting to remark that the bananas were not yet completely ripe – then, getting out my towel and walking on tip-toe so as not to wake up the neighbours, I would go into the bathroom – a large room with doors on either side, crammed with old furniture and wash-tubs, with the bath itself taking up only part of the space and partitioned off by screens hung with washing to dry, as were the numerous pieces of rope strung out across the room, so that it resembled the backstage of a theatre more than anything else.

In addition to Gilya the flat was inhabited by some other women: the elderly sisters, Khaya and Tsilya Markovna, stout the pair of them, with dyed red hair, and I never did learn to tell them apart, especially as they were so often visited by a third sister who lived somewhere on the outskirts – and they were all very good at cooking things like carrots in sweet sauce, cutlets, stuffed fish and pies, and strudels smelling of cinnamon – and then there was Lyora, the daughter of one of the two sisters, either of Khaya or Tsilya Markovna, a very plump spinster past her prime who worked as a nurse with the ambulance service and longed for a husband but who carefully and even proudly concealed this from others, in expectation of a happy twist of fate – and she would either be asleep or out, and through the open door of her room you could often see her bed, for some reason always uncovered with its enormous feather-pillow and a carelessly turned-back light-blue duvet – and finally Anna Dmitriyevna, a desiccated old woman who had once obviously been beautiful and imposing, with a shaking head and trembling hands who would help Gilya to keep house and who, together with her husband, a former White officer long since killed, had once owned the whole of this flat – and she would spend days on end sitting in her little box-room smoking Belomor *papirosas* with the television never off, never refusing a glass of vodka and a staunch supporter of Soviet rule, all of which caused constant irritation to Gilya who regarded Anna Dmitriyevna as a complete and utter fool.

And then after dinner I lay down on the sofa which was a little bit short for me causing my feet to hang over the end slightly, and the bolster was too high, but if I took it away, the position of my head would be uncomfortably low – and I lay there wrapped in the blanket which Gilya had thoughtfully prepared, reading a volume of Dostoyevsky taken at random from an old, pre-revolutionary edition of his collected works which stood in the book-case together with other editions, just as old, their grey and dark-blue covers embossed with gold – the remnants of books which survived the Blockade along with a whole library of books on urology, of no use to anyone and which lined the black book-shelves along the wall in the neighbouring room where, by this time, Gilya was getting ready to go to sleep – and she had preserved these books of Mozya's religiously, and just as religiously she would visit Mozya's grave on the anniversary of his birth or death or for no reason at all – he had died in Gilya's bed twenty-odd years ago – and in our family we used to call Moisey Ernstovich by the name of Mozya, because that is what Gilya used to call him – it must have been some variation on the German name: Moisey – Moses – Mozya, and anyway, he had studied in Germany somewhere, before the Revolution, as all Jews did who wanted to receive higher education – and it may even have been that his father also came under some German influence, since the name 'Ernst' was obviously a German one – and Mozya had been a fairly tall, smart-looking man, punctilious in the German way, completely bald with a small moustache and mocking black eyes surmounted by shaggy brows – a professor of urology in private practice who had played chess so magnificently in his youth that he had received his master's title, and who was generally regarded as a thrifty and even miserly person – and in '37 Mozya had been imprisoned but, thanks to the efforts of somebody or other, was quickly released – and Gilya would often relate this story in all its exciting detail – about his arrest, his imprisonment and his return – how there had been a sudden ring at her door late at night and she had gone to open it, thinking they had come for her – and it turned out to be Mozya – and, not believing her eyes, she had rushed towards him, together with her bosom friend El'za, who had done so much for her, living with her for practically the whole period Mozya was in jail and then calling her daughter Gil'da in honour of Gilya – yes, El'za was a loyal friend of the house, and it was Mozya who first discovered that she had breast-cancer, even though he was a urologist.

The light from the old-fashioned table-lamp with its green shade which had belonged to Mozya and stood permanently on his desk, was falling on to the pages of the book I was reading – the circle of light trembled as a tram passed by outside, and the house shook and vibrated very slightly, even though it was old and firmly built – and in the room next door you could just hear the sound of Gilya gulping down her sleeping-pill and then switching off the light over her bed – 'Are you still as keen on Dostoyevsky?' she would always ask me and, without waiting for an answer, would immediately add: 'Only don't talk about it at the Brodskys' – Brodsky was her former boss and, although she had given up work a long time ago, she continued to have friendly relations with him and all his family, but especially with his wife Dora Abramovna, a lean, energetic woman in charge not only of her whole numerous family but also of the administrative and research activities of the section which Brodsky headed – and the Brodskys would observe all the Jewish festivals, ate nothing that was not kosher and had been intending to emigrate to Israel for many years, but Brodsky's sons were engaged in some kind of secret work and he himself as an academician was afraid of any unnecessary stir which might be connected with his name – and that evening, as I lay on the short, broken sofa, listening to the lulling creak of nocturnal trams turning the corner next to Gilya's flat and then careering off down the snow-covered street, swaying from side to side as always happens with empty carriages when they speed along, heading somewhere into the distance where the lines of street-lamps merged in the gloom of the frosty night, I leafed through, in the slightly wavering circle of light cast by the bulb from beneath the green lamp-shade, the penultimate volume of Dostoyevsky's works, containing the *Diary of a Writer* for 1877 or 1878 – and finally I stumbled on an article especially devoted to the Jews – 'The Jewish Question' it was called – and I should not have been surprised to discover it because he was bound after all somewhere or other to have gathered together in one place all those 'Jews, Jewesses, Jew-boys and Yids' with which he so liberally besprinkled the pages of his novels – now as the poseur Lyamshin squealing with terror in *The Possessed*, now as the arrogant and at the same time

114

cowardly Isaiah Fomich in *Memoirs from the House of the Dead* who did not scruple to lend money at enormous interest to his fellow-convicts, now as the fireman in *Crime and Punishment* with that 'everlasting sullen grief, so sourly imprinted on all members of the tribe of Judah without exception', and with his laughable way of pronouncing Russian which is reproduced in the novel with such particular and fastidious pleasure, now as the Jew who crucified the Christian child and then cut off its finger, relishing the child's agony (Liza Khokhlakova's story in *The Brothers Karamazov*) – but most often he would depict them as nameless money-lenders, tight-fisted tradesmen or petty thieves who are not even fully portrayed but simply mentioned as little Jews or some other term implying the lowest and basest qualities of the human character – no, there was nothing surprising about the fact that the author of these novels should somewhere or other have finally expressed his views on this subject, have finally displayed his theory – although in fact there *was* no special theory – only fairly hackneyed arguments and myths (which have not lost their currency to this very day, incidentally): about the way Jews send gold and jewels to Palestine, about world Jewry which has ensnared practically the whole globe in its greedy tentacles, about the way Jews have mercilessly exploited and made drunkards of the Russian nation which makes it impossible to grant them equal rights, or else they would completely consume the Russian people etc. – and I read all this with a pounding heart, hoping to discover in these arguments, which you might have expected to hear from some member of the Black Hundreds, at least some ray of hope, at least some movement in the other direction, at least some effort to view the whole problem from a new angle – and not just that Jews should be allowed to profess only their religion and nothing else – and it struck me as being strange to the point of implausibility that a man so sensitive in his novels to the sufferings of others, this jealous defender of the insulted and the injured who fervently and even frenetically preached the right to exist of every earthly creature and sang a passionate hymn to each little leaf and every blade of grass – that this man should not have come up with even a single word in the defence or justification of a people persecuted over several thousands of years – could he have been so blind? – or was he perhaps blinded by hatred? – and he did not even refer to the Jews as a people, but as a tribe as though they were a group of natives from the Polynesian islands or somewhere – and to this tribe I belonged and the many friends and acquaintances of mine with whom I had discussed the subtlest problems of Russian literature, and to this tribe also belonged Leonid Grossman and Dolinin, Zil'bershtein and Rozenblyum, Kirpotin and Kogan, Fridlender and Bregova, Borshchevsky and Gosen-pud, Mil'kina and Hus, Zundelovich and Shklovsky, Belkin, Bergman and Dvosya L'vovna Sorkina and the many other Jewish literary critics who have gained what amounts almost to a monopoly in the study of Dostoyevsky's literary heritage – and there was something unnatural and at first glance even enigmatic in the passionate and almost reverential way in which they dissected and to this day continue to analyse the diaries, notebooks, rough drafts, letters and even pettiest biographical details of this man who despised and hated their race – perhaps it was a kind of cannibalistic act performed on the leader of an enemy tribe – but it is possible, however, that this special attraction which Dostoyevsky seems to possess for Jews reveals something else: the desire to hide behind his back, as if using him as a safe-conduct – something like adopting Christianity or daubing a cross on your door during a pogrom – although one cannot exclude the simple fervour of Jews here which has always been particularly strong in questions concerning Russian culture and the preservation of the Russian national spirit and which, in any case, completely accords with the preceding supposition.

Outside, the noise of the trams had already ceased, and I had long since turned out the light, placing Mozya's lamp carefully down on the dining-table – and in the next room Gilya's delicate snoring could be heard – ten breaths followed by a tiny snore – so tiny it was as if she was not snoring at all but sobbing in her sleep – and my feet just hung there over the edge of the sofa, and outside the window was the impenetrable, Petersburg, winter's night, and although it was very late, there was still a whole eternity to go until dawn – and you could lie there peacefully and not worry about having to get to sleep because it might soon be first light.

The lonely figure in narrow checked trousers, black top-hat and black Berlin frock-coat with flapping skirts and pockets bulging with sandwiches, flew along the snow-covered platform of some station between Baden-Baden and Basel, bobbing up and down, curtseying and performing absurd dancing steps, as he shouted something about being short-changed by a franc, but the train had long since gone and night had descended, and the man continued to run and bob and curtsey, shining brightly in some flood-light which persistently followed him, as if all this were taking place on a stage, and circling slowly in the shaft of light and falling were flakes of snow, covering his face and beard in a white shroud – and the platform came to an end, and he now ran along a tight-rope stretched across the dome of a circus tent, and the white shroud covering his face was the mask of Harlequin from which tufts of his grey beard protruded – and removing his top-hat, he would throw it up into the air and catch it in mid-flight, curtseying and executing all kinds of dance steps as he did so, and sitting below in the front row, following the movements of the illuminated figure on the tight-rope unremittingly, was a man with a large head, lion's mane and well-groomed beard, his coldly gleaming lorgnette placed against his eyes – and the figure in the Harlequin mask danced and juggled with his black top-hat solely for that person sitting in the front row – and coming to a halt on the tight-rope, he would lift one leg then the other like an actress in an operetta, as he hurled his jacket especially high into the air, almost reaching the tip of the roof, so that it looked as if the dancer on the tight-rope must almost certainly fall, but the face of the person watching him remained impenetrable, and only in the depths of his eyes behind the cold lenses of the lorgnette were there occasional fervent, encouraging flashes of green, and only when the dancer finally fell from the tight-rope and hurtled downwards, executing desperate pirouettes in the air as he did so, did the face of the person with the large head and the lion's mane light up with a smile – a charming, aristocratic, if somewhat arrogant, smile – and removing his lorgnette, he laughed and applauded approvingly – and the performer who had fallen from the tight-rope was running along the snow-covered platform again, but this was no longer a station somewhere between Baden-Baden and Basel, this was Tver', which lies in between Moscow and Petersburg – and with the skirts of his frock-coat flapping, the person running down the platform tried desperately to catch the travelling dignitaries who were stepping down from the express train to stretch their legs a little or to get a breath of fresh air – and he rushed from one official to another, trying desperately to grasp at a hand or catch a glance, humbly requesting something and bowing – and the dignitaries disappeared into a first-class carriage, and there he was trying to run after the train – and the platform was turning into a staircase which led to gaming-rooms – and he was climbing up the steps of a carpeted marble staircase, unhurriedly, looking nonchalant, and various Poles and Jews bustled about in front of him – and even Rothschild was nothing to him, because in a few minutes he himself might be richer than Rothschild, that skinflint of a Jew who had acquired his millions through money-lending, whereas he would gain his money from a fortunate concatenation of circumstances and nothing more, a happy coincidence which he could guess in advance, and in any case it was not the millions which were important to him, but the *idea* – and he nonchalantly pushed his way through the crowd of gamblers and onlookers – those poor, avaricious fools – haughtily staring at their yellow faces, desiccated by an unhealthy passion – and with his first bet he won half a million, then another million, but somebody gave his arm a painful tug – a man with a squashed face like a wash-tub and protruding ears who was giving him an insolent look, and beneath the gaze of those bulging eyes he suddenly sank to the floor and then crawled on all fours to the exit where he rolled down the stairs, bumping against every step, not feeling the pain and losing his top-hat in the process – and he walked up to the big looking-glass hanging in the entrance-hall to straighten his appearance, but instead of himself in the mirror he saw the puny figure of Isaiah Fomich, without any clothes on and with the breast of a chicken – and he recoiled, and, Isaiah Fomich recoiled, too – and then he started to bombard Isaiah Fomich with the sandwiches he had stuffed in his pockets at the station where he had shouted about the short-changed franc with the piercing scream of a money-lender who has been robbed, drowning out the whistle of the steam-engine, but the more he threw sandwiches at Isaiah Fomich, the clearer and more lifelike that feeble figure became.

When I woke up it was already light, if a little grey, and snowflakes were slowly circling down past the window – and I could hear careful steps in the corridor and Gilya's voice, which seemed to be giving Anna Dmitriyevna instructions about the housekeeping – and, stretching my hand out towards the chair, I looked at my watch – it was half past ten – a belated Petersburg winter's morning.

After breakfast, sitting down on Mozya's old sofa, I had a long chat with Gilya who asked me questions about my work and mutual acquaintances, told me about her former boss and the goings on between her former niece and her nephew who, after the divorce, had set up a new family, and although she, Gilya, had nothing against his new wife, she had no intention of setting foot in their house – and angry sparks appeared in Gilya's good-natured eyes, once brown and now faded, and her voice grew harder, changing its intonation and vocabulary, and it looked as if she would suddenly jump up and begin talking, or rather, shouting in Yiddish, as her parents used to do in the place near Kiev where she herself was born, but most interesting were her stories of the Leningrad Blockade, how people actually ate the dogs and cats, how she gave two beautiful lengths of cloth belonging to Mozya in exchange for a loaf of bread, and how Mozya, who was so weak he could scarcely get up, gained strength before her very eyes when she fed him with this bread as well as two chunks of horse-flesh which she had managed to get in the special retail establishment for

119

scientists, after she had spent a whole twenty-four hours standing in a queue, and how when going down Nevsky Prospect or crossing the Kirov Bridge, which she would do twice a day since the Institute where she worked was situated on Petrograd Side, she would see frozen corpses being dragged along on toboggans, and how people would collapse before her very eyes, freezing to death on the same spot, with their bodies either being picked up or not, in which case they would become frozen to the pavement or the roadway and remain lying there till the following spring.

But our most intimate conversations would usually take place in the evenings, after supper when it was beginning to get slightly gloomy outside, as if it were about to rain, but never became really dark because it was during the white nights, and the superfluous street-lights shone outside all night, which you knew had fallen only because the trams grew silent – and these conversations seemed particularly cosy during the long winter evenings, when there was no prospect of dawn and a blizzard raged outside the window, making the street-lights almost invisible, and somewhere down below you could hear the muffled grinding of trams at the corner – and I would be reclining on Mozya's sofa and Gilya would sit next to me telling stories, smoothly and in great detail (she had an excellent memory) about how her first boss, a famous chemist, had been imprisoned, and how he had been exiled to a special camp for scientists needed by the country, and how he had then, not very long before the war, been helped to get out of prison by Romain Rolland who had pleaded on his behalf practically as far as Stalin, and how this boss of hers, the famous chemist, had then been imprisoned a second time a few months later and had disappeared without trace – and then she would switch to the story of Mozya's arrest, about how he was interrogated by an investigator with a very Jewish-sounding surname, famed for his brutality even outside Leningrad, and about how Mozya returned home late one evening and she was dumbfounded to see him as was her friend E'lza who lived with her during that difficult period when Mozya was in prison.

It was getting dark now, too, – the short winter's day was coming to an end – in the street outside it was frosty, and the snow crunched under people's feet – and trams queued up behind the traffic-lights, the figures of people lit up by the street-lamps and the snow crowded around the bus and tram-stops or moved along the pavements – and men stood in small huddles outside the store at the corner waiting to form their drinking groups of three, and a little further away from the shop you could see other figures with pale, haggard faces – leaning against the walls of the building, which left traces of lime on their backs, until they slowly and inexorably slid down onto the pavement, lying prostrate until special cars with a red cross gathered them up – and I was walking along in the direction of Nevsky Prospect which I could already see shining in the distance, like a river during carnival time – in fact it *was* a river, Nevsky Prospect, flowing somewhere in the distance into the Neva – a tributary of it, straight and wide, dividing the whole Nevsky district of the city into two parts, one of which had once been aristocratic with its former Sergiyevskaya, Nadezhdinskaya, Basseinaya, Kirochnaya Streets and Voskresensky Prospect, irreproachable in their straightness and the severity of their buildings, with its Square of the Arts, almost unnatural within the miraculous perfection of the architectural complex surrounding it, with its Field of Mars instinct with some kind of spirit of sorrow and solemnity, and the Engineers' Palace lying adjacent to it with its pointed towers and inaccessible inner courtyards and annexes, guardians of some terrible secret, with its Fontanka and Moyka Embankments, slightly curving and lined with buildings, most of them adorned with memorial plaques, with its Cathedral of Christ of the Blood whose red and gold cupola suddenly appears in view from the most unexpected places, with its former Millionaya Street, lined with many-storeyed aristocratic residences with moulded cornices and plate-glass windows, that precursor or portent of the English Embankment, lined no longer with private villas but palaces overlooking the frighteningly wide and slightly convex surface of the Neva, as broad as an estuary, the English

Embankment running then into the Palace Embankment with the Winter Palace, the former heart of the Russian Empire, dissected into a museum exhibit – and then there is the other half of the district, once plebeian, with streets not always submitting to rectilinear order and occasionally diverging into side-streets and cul-de-sacs cut by the narrow, capriciously twisting Catherine Canal – all those former Bol'shaya, Srednyaya and Malaya Meshchanskaya Streets or Stolyarny Lane, lined with four- and five-storeyed tenements – a whole labyrinth of streets, suddenly thrown up against the railings lining the Catherine Canal, a labyrinth all the more confusing in that I was anxious not to mistake the street or the number of the building supposed to appear before my camera lens when, driven on by lack of time, the fickleness of the Leningrad weather or the threat of being stopped for filming unsuitable subjects, I would wander around, taking photographs of the Raskol'nikov House or the Old Moneylender's House or Sonechka's House or buildings where their author had lived during the darkest and most clandestine period of his life in the years immediately following his return from exile – and it was precisely here, at this corner house on the Catherine Canal, that he was visited by the woman with the veil pulled down low over her face (the one he later did not dare to touch as they journeyed together in the same cabin) before the appearance of Anna Grigor'yevna who came to visit him in one of the buildings in this confused labyrinth of streets intersected by the canal, forestalling her student rival as she climbed up the narrow marble staircase to the second floor, seated herself with eyes modestly lowered at the little round table in his study and began to take down *The Gambler* as he dictated, feeling his eyes on her, listening to his footsteps, to the sound of him circling round her, her heart missing a beat whenever he approached, until he stung her so exquisitely.

When I emerged on to Nevsky, it looked exactly like a river, a river in the middle of a winter carnival – gliding up and down it in the frosty mist were hundreds of lights, red, green and orange, infinitely reflected on its silvery, icy surface, and moving along its 'embankments', up and down the wide pavements on either side of the prospect, were crowds of people, illuminated in the blazing shop-windows and enveloped time and again in the clouds of frosty steam which emanated from the doors of shops and restaurants whenever they were thrown open, and blazing and dancing above all this were the multi-coloured neon advertisements, swathed in the same frosty steam clouds which managed to drift up to them – and at a wink from the traffic-signals the lights slipping up and down the frozen prospect would come to a momentary halt, and then the crowds would stream across the 'bridges' to the other side – and, finding myself on the other side, too, I entered a side-street which, after the wild orgy of lights on Nevsky, seemed so dark and quiet with only two lines of street-lamps stretching away somewhere into the distance, disappearing in the darkness – and when I looked at the street-sign placed on one of the buildings, it turned out that I was walking along Marat, formerly Nikolayevskaya, Street – and somewhere around here, not very far from Nevsky, perhaps on the very spot where I now walked, he had been overtaken by some drunken lout dressed in a sheepskin coat who punched him in the face with his fist – and this was nearly two years before his death, as he was returning home after his usual late afternoon walk – and he was knocked to the ground, his cap rolling along over the roadway which was still covered with snow as it was the end of March – and a crowd collected around him, people helped him to his feet, there was blood on his face, and the policeman who had run up took the drunken man to the police-station together with a few witnesses – and a few days later the trial took place, and the offender was sentenced to a fine of sixteen roubles – the victim being present and begging the court to be lenient towards the miscreant and pardon him – and he waited for his assailant near the door and, when he came out of the court-room, thrust the sixteen roubles into his hand – and at this period in his life he had been writing a particularly prolific amount about the Slavonic Question, emphasizing the God-given role of the Russian people whose vocation it was to free the rest of Europe, the basis of this chosen destiny being, in his opinion, the special, unique nature of the Russian national mentality and character which, amongst other things, was demonstrated in the use of unprintable words, pronounced in various ways and with various shades of meaning, which were employed by the common people not, of course, to insult others or abuse them, but to express the subtle, profound and even saintly feelings buried in the soul of every genuine Russian.

The pavement I walked along was heaped with snow on both sides, the crunch made by the feet of lone pedestrians being occasionally interrupted by the sound of passing cars, raising a flurry of snow behind them – and although the street had now come to an end, I walked on at random, led by a kind of instinct – first to the left, then to the right, and then straight ahead once again along snowy streets just as quiet, lined with identical four- and five-storeyed tenement buildings with dimly lit windows and entrance-ways as deep and dark as wells – and the main thing at the end of the day was to keep parallel with the Ligovka and not diverge from it – and then suddenly I nearly ran straight into a dark, squat, two-storeyed building with locked gates, and rising up to my right was the dimly visible, gigantic white edifice of a church, its cupolas disappearing into the black sky – in front of me was the Kuznechny Market, and to the right and behind me the Vladimir Church – I had reached exactly the right spot, and my heart was pounding with joy and some other vaguely sensed feeling – and to the left of the Kuznechny Market, right opposite and across the street where I was standing, was a four-storeyed building with a semi-basement which almost gave the impression that it had five storeys, a grey-coloured, corner building which appeared black in the darkness – and the corner of the building was not sharp, but truncated, as with many similar Petersburg structures, and this flat corner wall was filled with windows and balconies one on top of the other above a door reached by a flight of steps leading into an entrance-hall and cloak-room placed in the semi-basement – and sitting at a table next to another door leading to a staircase was a woman selling tickets, and these tickets you could keep as souvenirs or throw away later because nobody checked them – and apart from this she had on offer a modest guide to the museum with a miserable reproduction of the writer's portrait and the furniture of his study along with a few sentences and a quotation from Saltykov-Shchedrin, and also on sale was a rectangular metal badge with a relief-engraving of his face and the bumps on his forehead – and the staircase took you into a large auditorium used for lectures and films or for actors to declaim his works, while the first and second floors contained a whole series of rooms with impeccably polished parquet floors smelling faintly of wax as in a church, containing an exhibition devoted to the memory of his life and works – and glass exhibition cases and various fixed or revolving stands contained photocopies of his letters, first editions of his works, portraits and photographs of him, members of his family and his contemporaries, cuttings from newspapers about contemporary Petersburg events, large photo-reproductions of Petersburg views and the fortress in Omsk, as well as Florence, Rome and Geneva (places he visited during his foreign travels), illustrations to his novels, shots of scenes from theatrical adaptations of his works, and a whole host of other documents.

An almost churchlike silence reigned in the museum, interrupted only by the reverent whisperings of a few couples who had wandered in, or by the rustling of pages as some lone, pimply youth diligently jotted something down in his notebook, and also by the dry crackle of fluorescent lights thoughtfully switched on by the elderly female attendants who tore themselves away from their knitting for a moment whenever one of the visitors found himself in a place where illumination was necessary – but, now and again, the museum's silence was broken by an unexpectedly loud voice, confidently explaining something – a group of schoolchildren approaching with their guide, the group adhering strictly to a predetermined plan of inspection as the guide's pointer slipped quickly over exhibits judged to be of secondary interest, lingered long over objects which possessed, from the guide's point of view, serious cognitive significance – and the schoolboys standing furthest away from the guide were pulling each other by the sleeve, peeking around from side to side and giggling – and the guides usually came down from the upper floor where the management and the research department were situated, the director being a youngish woman with a resonant Tartar Christian name and the surname of a famous general whose wife she had been, beautiful with a roundish face and long, shining, black slit-eyes – and she was always busy in her office with representatives of various bureaucratic organizations, occasionally stunning them with some metaphysical question or suddenly surprising them by changing the subject to the state of her health, while next door, in the research section, the museum employees, young men and women with educated faces, making you think instinctively that they must be of Jewish origin, were exchanging the latest literary gossip and constantly ringing people up on the telephone, and then, to the friendly laughter of the others, one of those who had been on the phone began to recount how a certain well-known actor (also with a Jewish surname, incidentally) who gave public readings of Dostoyevsky's stories and often performed in the auditorium at the museum, had spent half the day lying in the bath while his wife told everyone over the phone that he wasn't in – and then one of his colleagues suggested he ring up again and ask whether the man had drowned yet – and this made everyone laugh all over again, and then the director suddenly entered and they began to recount the story, and everyone could see that she wanted to laugh along with them, but she put on a severe expression and asked someone a question about work, being given a reply, but not a serious one somehow, and people even began a discussion on her favourite metaphysical topics, but in a semi-joking way in the form of particular remarks or phrases well-known to everyone as a trade-mark of hers, and she tried to brush them aside with mock severity but in the end could not keep it up any more and burst into laughter along with them.

And it was here on this second floor, if you count the semi-basement as a floor, that his flat was situated – and in a special stand in the entrance-hall was an umbrella with a big splayed wooden handle and slightly faded black canvas, the supposition being that this was the umbrella which he used to take with him on walks, and hanging on a peg was a very old wide-brimmed hat (could this really have been his?) – and in the first room, the sitting-room, I think, were some old book-cases full of books and two or three neat little ladies' tables with inlaid work gone dark with age and some lattice-work down below (not unlike Gilya's table) – and lying on one of the tables was a sheet of paper torn from an exercise-book with a few phrases on it written in a clumsy, childish hand and signed: 'Lyuba' – and on the walls were family photographs of Anna Grigor'yevna, by herself and with the children, Lyuba and Fedya – and in one of the photographs taken after their father's death the eleven-year-old Lyuba looks like a mature, fully-grown young lady, which is particularly emphasized by her loosened hair and the long dress concealing her shoes – and just a few years after her father's death she parted from her mother and set up house by herself, something not unlike a salon where she lived an extremely wayward existence, so much so that Anna Grigor'yevna, seeing a young girl's coffin being carried out of church on one occasion, was heard to exclaim: 'Now, why couldn't that be my daughter they are carrying out!' and a few years after that Lyubov' Fyodorovna went abroad, partly as a result of her profound lack of psychological balance, perhaps, indeed, mental illness – but nonetheless, in the intervals between her regular attacks of depression she managed to write her memoirs of her father, which Dostoyevsky scholars do not take too seriously, regarding many of the 'facts' she adduces as being unconvincing, and her arguments as superficial and subjective – and in particular, they regard her attempt to prove the Norse origins of Dostoyevsky as some obsessive idée fixe – and one person particularly zealous in this direction was the scholar Gornfel'd, who wrote an introduction to Lyubov' Fyodorovna's books in which he declares the slightest doubt about Dostoyevsky's being part of the Russian nation as anathema, almost as a personal insult – and the son, Fedya, however, in this photograph resembled more a diligent but rather dense little high-school boy with a kind of degenerate-shaped head, almost a malicious caricature of his father's skull – and then there was another room of some kind, which possibly belonged to Anna Grigor'yevna, also containing photographs and even a few pictures on the wall, and a small desk – and then, further on, another room of sorts, nothing very remarkable, leading to his study with its desk covered in books and manuscripts as well as *papirosa* papers and a tobacco-box, two burnt-out candles, an inkstand and a desk calendar left open at the date of his death – and next to the desk was a book-case filled with books which, according to the version of events recounted by Anna Grigor'yevna in her *Memoirs*, played a fateful part in bringing about the pulmonary haemorrhage which began one night when he tried moving it to retrieve his pen-holder which had fallen down the back.

The bleeding, however, which had quickly come to a halt, started up again with renewed force the following day when, according to Anna Grigor'yevna's account, Fyodor Mikhaylovich became particularly irritated by one of his frequent visitors, a very good-natured man, but an inveterate arguer, although in her *Memoirs* she also passes over in silence the visit that day from Fedya's favourite sister, Vera Mikhaylovna, who had come from Moscow specially to discuss the question of the inheritance – and this was the same sister who once used to live on Staraya Basmannaya Street in the Institute of Surveying and whose family she and Fedya had visited at Shrove-tide soon after their marriage, when they had arrived in Moscow, staying in the room at the Hotel Dussot with a view over the snow-covered cupolas of the Moscow churches and the white-blanketed street below with its hurtling sledges and carriages harnessed with troikas of horses – and taking one of these sledges and covering themselves over with the fur blanket, they had ridden across the whole of Moscow, stopping outside the churches which Fedya, who knew Moscow well, showed her as if they were his own – and stepping down from the sledge, he would genuflect and, removing his hat, cross himself in the direction of the church, and she would do likewise after him, and then in Vera Mikhaylovna's drawing-room she would stoically put up with the hostile looks of her hostess and her entire family who had been intending Fedya to marry some relative of theirs, meeting their looks and gibes head-on, glowering back at them and, with a purposely indifferent air, smoothing out the flounces on her dress, although her fingers trembled against her will and crumpled the fabric, as she felt that the mast, which was her salvation and which she gripped onto so as not to be washed away by the sea, was about to slip from her grasp – and she had withstood all these glances and caustic remarks, pressing herself to the mast ever more firmly, and she never could forget this first encounter with his Moscow relatives who were quite up to the standard of his Petersburg ones – that Pasha with his impertinent grin and Emiliya Fyodorovna, the wife of his already deceased brother Mikhail, with her sharp, little, coal-black eyes, both of whom were hostile to Anna Grigor'yevna from the very beginning, regarding her as some kind of obstacle, considering that Fedya should be devoting his whole life to helping *them*, although Emiliya Fyodorovna had grown-up children who were perfectly able to support her, and Pasha was simply an idler with no desire to work and who only served to bring blushing shame upon Fedya, whenever he tried to arrange some kind of work for his stepson – but Fedya still continued to help him – the first time actually before they went abroad, when Pasha and Emiliya Fyodorovna literally tried to stop them from going, physically barring their exit from the room and demanding money, forcing Fedya to pawn his only overcoat, and it was only thanks to Anna Grigor'yevna's angel of a mother, who gave money to the stepson and the sister-in-law, as well as to Fedya and herself, that they succeeded in escaping from Petersburg at that time and preserving their family – then, after they returned from abroad, when all their property had been distrained because of his dead brother's debts to do with the tobacco factory, Fedya had met ten thousand roubles' worth of bills, some of which turned out to be bogus, and as a result of all this the publishing enterprise, earlier set up together with his brother, had gone into shameful liquidation and Fedya himself had nearly been sent to debtors' prison – though by this time, it is true, she had already taken affairs into her own hands and had begun to give short shrift to those leeches of creditors, though here, too, she wouldn't have managed without the financial help of her mother – apart from Emiliya Fyodorovna and Pasha, it was a question every month of paying fifty roubles to Fedya's ailing drunkard of a brother, Nikolay – and in general Fedya could never refuse money to anybody, in fact, giving alms to every beggar he met, sometimes to the same one several times a day, with the result that once in Staraya Russa Anna Grigor'yevna had dressed herself and the children up in shawls and taken up position along the route which Fedya usually followed – 'Kind sir,' she had said, when Fedya had come up to them, 'I've got a sick husband and two children,' and Fedya had immediately given alms to his own wife – and then she burst into merry laughter, and he flew into a rage, regarding what she had done as something blasphemous – 'It's the same as placing a stone in a beggar's outstretched hand!' he had shouted, as they all walked together in the direction of the dock, 'except that here it's the other way round, but that's not the point! It amounts to mocking man's finest feelings, do you understand?' – shouting so loudly that people had already begun to look round at them, but Anna Grigor'yevna had not felt the slightest bit guilty because over the last few years he had simply become a spendthrift with this alms-giving of his, almost forcing himself on others to the point of becoming a laughing-stock, even to those who benefited from his charity – and there was something unnatural about this, something hysterical, as if he were atoning for former sins or attempting to suppress some contrary feeling within himself, perhaps even some instinct – it was all turning into some kind of penitential madness – but the main thing was that he was giving away money here, there and everywhere without worrying about the fact that Anna Grigor'yevna scarcely had enough to keep them going and they still had unpaid debts and Anna Grigor'yevna, who had set up a book business, had to stay up late at night writing and sealing envelopes to customers and checking the accounts as well as running the household, and they had children who had to receive some kind of legacy after they had gone – and the only ray of hope in all this, like a patch of light glimmering dimly at the end of a long corridor, was the inheritance they would receive from his Aunt Kumanina in Moscow, according to which Fedya and the other relatives would share a 1500 acre estate near Ryazan' with a splendid timber forest, and although Fedya appeared little interested by this, Anna Grigor'yevna had tried to explain to him that this was the only reliable security for their future and, more important, for the future of their children, and he surprised himself by suddenly realizing that this was in fact the case and he would even see himself occasionally almost as a landowner showing his ancestral estate off to his friends and acquaintances or even imagine himself as some agricultural or economic luminary, although such thoughts were idle and he tried to suppress the temptation to think them – and it was just at this time that it became known that his favourite sister, Vera Mikhaylovna, who lived in Moscow, was about to visit Petersburg on a special mission: that of requesting Fedya to renounce his share of Aunt Kumanina's legacy in favour of his sisters, and when Anna Grigor'yevna heard about this, the patch of light glimmering dimly somewhere at the end of a long, dark corridor was extinguished, and when Fedya began to say something about his dear sisters, and especially about Vera Mikhaylovna, for whom since childhood he had nurtured the deepest affection, she went pale and, glowering at him with a cold, alien stare, declared, articulating each word clearly and distinctly: 'There's a benefactor of humanity for you! Always dancing to his relations' tune!' – and he went pale, too, and for a few days afterwards was very reserved with Anna Grigor'yevna, scarcely speaking to her, and when Vera Mikhaylovna arrived in Petersburg and came to them for lunch in the dim light of a Petersburg winter's day, he pointedly addressed himself only to her, as if Anna Grigor'yevna did not exist at all, questioning her assiduously about their Moscow relations and mutual friends, although Vera Mikhaylovna seemed distracted, giving monosyllabic answers, and as soon as soup was served, she immediately got down to business, explaining to her brother how advantageous it would be for him because, when he had renounced his share of the property, he would receive his portion in money, and in any case, considering how overwhelmed he always was with work, it wouldn't exactly be easy for him to travel to Ryazan' Province, and besides the journey would swallow up a great deal of money and time – and he sat there, saying nothing, staring down in front of him as he rolled a tiny ball of bread between his fingers – he had scarcely touched his soup, feeling Anna Grigor'yevna's expectant gaze upon him, and when the second course was served, Vera Mikhaylovna suddenly put down her knife and fork and, producing a cambric handkerchief, began to blow her nose very loudly and then burst into tears, and dabbing the handkerchief to her eyes, she began telling him that, if he did not agree, it would be an inhuman way for him to treat his sisters – and without looking at Anna Grigor'yevna, he could feel her searching eyes upon him, and this gaze seemed to be both reproving and mocking – 'For God's sake, leave me in peace, all of you!' he shouted, pushing the plate with its steaming main course away from him – and with his napkin still tucked in behind his collar, he jumped up from the table and walked swiftly over towards his study, slammed the door, sat down at his desk and buried his head in his hands, his heart beating loudly, pounding away like a hammer in his ears – and from the dining-room or drawing-room or somewhere came the sound of hushed voices, gradually receding, probably Anna Grigor'yevna accompanying his sister to the door – and the reunion with his sister, the family lunch which he had so much anticipated, buying those particular sweetmeats his sister had loved since she was a child – all this was ruined – it served them right! – and he wanted to hurl something, to smash something, to make things even worse – and then suddenly he could feel some sticky liquid on the palms of his hands – it was almost dark in the room – and with trembling hands he lit one of the two candles standing on his desk and jumped up off his chair in horror – both his hands were covered in blood, as if he had just committed a murder – and automatically he ran his hand over his beard, probably to wipe it, but the blood on his palm only increased – and he grabbed hold of the starched napkin which he had tucked into his collar during lunch – it was damp and as red as a railway lineman's warning flag – and still not believing that this was actually happening to *him*, but realizing that something irreparable had taken place, he rushed to the study door, threw it wide open and, with all his strength, cried out: 'Anya!' – and although his voice came out weakly, she heard it at the other end of the flat, in the entrance-hall where, apologizing for all that had happened, she had just seen Vera Mikhaylovna to the door – and she ran through the rooms, not noticing the children, bumping into furniture, because she could sense that something terrible had happened – and through the two days that remained of his life he scarcely left his couch upholstered in black leather which is nowadays cordoned off from the rest of the study by a ribbon (although not the original, received by the museum from someone in the Dostoyevsky family), with the photograph of the 'Sistine Madonna' above, given to him by one of his friends and hung in his study by Anna Grigor'yevna on his birthday – and his usual doctor arrived, examined him and said that there was no direct threat to the patient's life, but soon after he had gone, the patient began to haemorrhage once again and for a short time even lost consciousness – and when he came round, he asked Anna Grigor'yevna, who was kneeling beside the couch, to summon the priest so he could make his confession and receive communion – and the priest appeared without delay because the Vladimir Church, whose cupolas were disappearing, as I looked at them now, into the black winter sky, was very close by – and Anna Grigor'yevna spent the whole night in her husband's study, settling herself somehow or other in the armchairs, scarcely closing her eyes, going up to him time and time again, as he slept, to adjust his quilt or to feel his forehead.

It was a clear winter's morning, but something hinted imperceptibly at the nearness of spring, whether it was the blueness of the sky, with its almost summery tint of azure which was partly visible through the window of the study, or the clamorous voices of the tradesmen and stallholders setting up their wares in the alleyway beneath their windows, or the particular modulations of the bells of the Vladimir Church – and he ate some white bread and caviare and drank some milk and cranberry fruit drink which Anna Grigor'yevna's mother had prepared for him, while Anna Grigor'yevna herself slipped off to the shop for a moment and got him choice grapes which at that time of year were not always easy to buy – and as she ran back up the stairs, for some reason she suddenly remembered how he used to buy grapes for her in Baden-Baden, especially those black ones, which they had eaten in the railway carriage as they departed, remembered him running the length of the platform clutching sandwiches with the train about to leave at any moment – and sitting beside the couch, she spread a starched napkin over his chest and fed him from a plate of grapes, and it seemed to her that every grape which he ate was infusing him with new strength, returning him to life – and during the course of the day a large number of visitors came to see him – from the editorial office, from the censors' department, and then there were the organizers of the forthcoming Pushkin evening when he was supposed to give an address, and simply people concerned about his health – and he even managed to dictate a few short business letters to her, on several occasions becoming irritable, becoming the old Fedya once more, as she rushed headlong to fulfil his caprices, but when this deceptive day approached its end and she put the children to bed early and went up to the next floor to ask the gentleman who lived there not to pace around his room because this always irritated Fedya, and when she had written a few shorthand entries in her diary and then made up a straw-mattress on the floor next to the couch on which the sick man was lying – by the time she had done all this, night had fallen, his last night in this house and this world – and she woke up several times and, lighting the candle, stared into his face – it was pale, but he was breathing peacefully and evenly, which reassured her, and she went back to sleep again, but in the morning, when she opened her eyes, he was already awake, head turned to look at her with something in his gaze which made her heart sink – 'I shall die today, Anya,' he said quietly, continuing to look at her in the same way – and she went up to him and, taking his hands in hers, began trying to convince him that things would turn out all right and that the doctors did not consider his condition dangerous, but pushing her hands to one side and continuing to whisper, because he was unable to speak loudly, he asked her to pass him the copy of the Gospels given to him by the wives of the Decembrists when he had been in penal servitude and which he always kept with him, covering it with many pencil marks in the margins – and opening it at random without looking down at the page, he asked her to read out loud the third verse from the top, and she read: 'And Jesus answering said unto him, Suffer it to be so now: for thus it becometh us to fulfil all righteousness' – 'You see,' he said, ' "Suffer it to be so now", so I shall die' – and he shut the book, and Anna Grigor'yevna, kneeling down beside him, took his hand in hers once again and he put her hand to his lips, kissing it, and then he fell asleep, breathing peacefully and evenly, and she stayed there kneeling, afraid to move in case she should wake him up, and when he did wake up, it was already late morning, and he wound up his watch himself, then he asked her to let him clean his teeth and to help him get dressed, and when he began to comb his hair, attempting to make it cover his bald patch, and Anna Grigor'yevna, fearing that it would cost him too much effort, took the comb from him and tried to do it for him herself, he became irritable and started to ask very loudly, even shouting, why she was doing it from the wrong side, so that, although she was afraid that this loud display of temper might not be any good for him, at the same time she was glad to see his irritable reaction, which gave her hope that he might recover since it was so characteristic of him, but when, with her help, he had nearly got himself completely dressed and was about to pull on his socks, blood appeared on his lips and chin once again – so she immediately put him back to bed, wiping the blood from his lips and beard with a towel – and he lay there fully dressed on his black leather couch and made no further attempt to get up.

There was a never-ending stream of visitors throughout the day, but Anna Grigor'yevna tried not to let them into the room, apart from doctors who came and went, feeling his pulse and listening to his breathing, shrugging their shoulders uncertainly in response to Anna Grigor'yevna's questioning look as she accompanied them out to the entrance-hall – and it had been gloomy from first thing in the morning, with two candles burning on the desk in his study the whole day, as though he was sitting and working there and had only slipped out for a minute or lain down for a short rest – and Anna Grigor'yevna scarcely left his side, kneeling down beside him and holding his hand in hers – by now he was scarcely able to lift his head – and round about the middle of this day, which was almost indistinguishable from night, Pasha arrived, and Anna Grigor'yevna could hear him talk to someone on the other side of the door about summoning the notary, and the sick man also heard his voice apparently, because he nodded his head in the direction of the key-hole, implying that Pasha might be spying on them, but all the same he allowed him to be admitted – and Pasha entered with silent footsteps and, going up to his stepfather, bent over towards his hand, but the man lying on the couch jerked it away and shook his head as an indication that he no longer wanted to see Pasha, and then, in a scarcely audible voice, he asked for the children to be sent for so that he might take his leave of them, and Anna Grigor'yevna led them into the room, and they were perhaps to remember for the whole of their lives the tickling feeling of their father's beard when, confused and frightened, and urged on by Anna Grigor'yevna, they went up close to the couch and, following their mother's example, knelt down at his bedside, and he, turning his head towards them, kissed them on their foreheads – first Lyuba, then Fedya – and then, raising his hand, he made the sign of the cross over them, and when the children had gone, he closed his eyes and lay there without moving, so that Anna Grigor'yevna suddenly thought that he had stopped breathing – 'Are you asleep?' she asked quietly, bending right over him – and he opened his eyes, and she saw in them once again the expression which she had glimpsed that morning, suddenly realizing that this expression was one of anguished despair, and that he would die, and a bitter lump came into her throat and, so as not to burst into sobbing in his presence, she left the study and gave free rein to her tears for a moment, letting her head fall on to the desk in her room, so that her hair, always painstakingly arranged, spread out over the desk, covering her hands – but she was unable to really cry, and for that reason her sobbing was more like laughter or the beginning of hysterics – and the children looked at her in terror and Maria, the cook, an elderly woman with a pock-marked face tied round with a kerchief, was standing in the doorway, fidgeting from one leg to the other, and from the entrance-hall and the sitting room could be heard the subdued hum of voices and the sound of coughing – the various friends, acquaintances and callers were gradually filling the flat, and some of them, carefully opening the door of her room and slipping quietly in, stopped some distance away from the weeping woman and began to exchange whispers about something – so, brushing away her tears and adjusting her hair, she walked quickly, almost ran into the dying man's room – how could she have left him alone, even for a moment? – and he was lying there in the same position, his eyes open and staring at the ceiling as though he was trying to read something there – sometimes he would whisper something, but his speech seemed disconnected: 'How unfair they are!' (perhaps about his sisters) . . . 'Don't make a draught' (possibly to Anna Grigor'yevna) . . . 'Has Maria shut the stove? . . . Is there enough? . . . How I am ruining you . . .' – and all this, as well as the arrival of Grigorovich and other events, Anna Grigor'yevna, albeit in a rather fragmentary fashion, none-theless managed to enter in her diary – after his death, it is true, but during that same evening – and despite everything, she did not lose her head, nor, as people like to say today, did she lose control of events – she sent for the doctors, settled up with the cab-drivers, sent Maria for some ice which, according to the doctor's instructions, the patient was to

137

swallow – she refused to allow the notary to come to the house, about which Pasha was so insistent, she informed the visitors about the state of her husband's health, and she even signed two or three business documents.

It was about seven o'clock in the evening, and she had changed the two candles on his desk because the others had already burned down, when his lips and chin began to dribble with blood once again – and she wiped the blood away with the towel hanging in the same place on the back of a chair, and, summoning Maria, managed with her help to place another cushion beneath his head to incline him higher, as his customary doctors, Koshlakov and von Bretzel, were recommending as they stood nearby, taking it in turns to feel his pulse, putting their stethoscopes to his chest occasionally and giving each other meaningful glances – and a tiny rivulet of blood flowed from the corner of his mouth again, as though he were wounded in the chest – and although Anna Grigor'yevna wiped it away, as soon as she removed the towel, the flow of blood appeared again in the same place, as though she had done nothing – there was no way of stopping the renewed haemorrhage now, and a little blood even spilled on to the pillow – and she knelt down next to his couch once again, holding him by the hand, bending over him slightly, resembling the figure of the sorrowing woman often depicted on gravestones – and he lay there, eyes closed, not opening them even at her call, as she quietly but distinctly repeated his name – he seemed to have lapsed into unconsciousness, and in the neighbouring rooms the restrained voices of the visitors could be heard and, again and again, cautious rings at the front door bell – as she stroked his hand gently, she would suddenly begin to think that it was only another fit, as had happened to him so many times, and that he simply had not yet recovered consciousness, and that at any moment he would open his eyes, recognize her and ask her to help him get up, and sometimes she would think it was all simply a dream and that she would wake up at any moment and hear him walking around in his study and the spoon clink in his glass, because he would often walk around holding a glass filled with strong tea, but the voices in the neighbouring rooms were becoming more and more audible and distinct – she could already hear the movement of feet, somebody's footsteps, getting ever clearer and closer – most likely the visitors were beginning to enter the study, and she realized with horror that this was actually happening and that she was on her knees before her dying husband, her husband, Fedya, who used to come to her every evening to say goodnight, used to write long, passionate and incoherent letters to her from Bad Ems, where he would travel every summer to take the cure, who used to cause jealous scenes at readings of his works whenever she exchanged a quick word with anyone or he thought she was looking at someone, and then they would walk home separately, but he would not be able to keep it up, and he would catch up with her and ask her to forgive him, saying that if she refused, then he would throw himself on his knees before her there and then – and she would forgive him, and they would walk on together – and supporting her carefully by the arm, he would look into her eyes and then, leaving her for a moment, would dash into a shop and buy her some sweetmeats – nuts, raisins, bon-bons – and when they arrived home, they would drink tea and he would produce the sweetmeats for her and the children, but if she had a cold, he would get irritated and ask her to stop sneezing, and this made her laugh, and in the end he would start to laugh as well.

The visitors had already invaded the room of the dying man and were crowding around in a mournful semi-circle at the opposite end of the study, not yet daring to approach the couch on which he lay, but the kneeling woman, the embodiment of sorrow, could feel the breath of these strangers who by some unwritten but inexorable law were now gaining a right to her husband – and in their presence she could not even allow herself to cry and she dropped her head on the dying man's hand in impotence – and someone began to try and persuade her to get up off her knees and at least take a little respite, someone who obligingly placed a chair behind her and carefully helped her to her feet – and reflected in the windows of the study were the trembling flames of the two candles standing on the desk and the photograph of the 'Sistine Madonna' floating in the clouds with the Child, which was hanging above the couch on which the dying man lay, and outside the windows was the wintry Petersburg night – just as it looked now at this moment most probably, with the same snow-covered streets and the same nocturnal sky into which vanished the cupolas of the Vladimir Church, but when Anna Grigor'yevna heard someone's light steps approaching her and saw her mother, she was unable to hold out any longer and she burst into sobs, pressing her head to her mother's breast, and her mother was unable to contain herself either and began to cry, and standing next to the dying man was Doctor Koshlakov, bending over him slightly, feeling his weakening pulse and looking at his large silver watch from time to time, as if this were able to alter something, the light of the candle flames falling straight onto the dying man's face, so white that it would have merged with the pillow, if it had not been for the dark shadows which had formed around the eyes and the beard, making it seem black – and he lay there in the suit which Anna Grigor'yevna had helped him put on that morning, like a person who has just received a mortal wound – his chest rising and falling convulsively, and audible from within, a continuous gurgling sound which would rise to his throat and burst through to the surface emerging from his mouth and nose in the form of bloody foam, and Anna Grigor'yevna, once more kneeling down by the couch, had that sudden, momentary thought again that he had just had a fit, because after a fit, bloodstained foam nearly always appeared on his mouth and a gurgling sound would come from his chest, and she was convinced that all this would pass, and that he would open his eyes at any moment and call her name, but the crowd of visitors, forming a semi-circle and occupying nearly half the room, was creeping inexorably closer, and moving at the head of all those onlookers was the tall and white-haired Grigorovich, that 'little Frenchy', as he had recently been christened by the dying man when, at one of his literary readings, he had noticed Grigorovich kissing Anna Grigor'yevna's hand –

this was one of those jealous scenes which he brought on Anna Grigor'yevna in the final years of his life – and having never particularly like Grigorovich in any case, after this incident he began to refer to him maliciously and spitefully, calling him a liar and a braggart for some reason and unceremoniously avoiding his company – but this may also have been the result of some insight which had come to him later in life, or was perhaps only a vague conjecture – and in those long ago times when the Panayev crowd had been persecuting him, it was precisely Grigorovich who lived with him then, acting the part of protector and almost of benefactor to him, delivering *Poor Folk* to Nekrasov, it was precisely Grigorovich who, as was later revealed for certain by Avdot'ya Panayeva's memoirs, being a sociable man, conveyed to the Panayev circle – Turgenev, Nekrasov and Belinsky – the fervent and passionate words uttered in an upsurge of frankness to someone who was his well-wisher and practically his room-mate by the author of *Poor Folk* and who would then report back the derisive and occasionally venomous comments of these people about *him*, thereby lighting and fanning the flames of enmity – and Grigorovich's mother really had been a Frenchwoman and even, it seems, an actress or dancer into the bargain, and the young Grigorovich, tall, longlegged and something of a playboy, was always the organizer and leading light of balls, performing the most subtle and difficult steps with uncommon ease, leading all the couples after him in the quadrille, going on one knee before his partner with particular elegance and skill – and at this moment he seemed to be more or less conducting things, too, stepping to the right slightly at one moment and drawing the crowd of visitors along after him, standing on tip-toe, almost on point, the next, moving with a few aerial steps in the direction of the couch, the visitors obeying his signal and moving forward, too, although Anna Grigor'yevna may only have imagined this because she was kneeling beside the couch with her head bowed over the face of the dying man and unable to see what was happening in the room behind her – she could only sense and surmise, and besides which, to judge by the fragmentary entries in her diary, Grigorovich called in during the daytime, but then, why should so refined and companionable a person as he *not* have stayed to see things through to the end, especially as he had been a friend of the dying man?

Anna Grigor'yevna's mother was now seated on a chair, her hands placed on the shoulders of her daughter who knelt at the head of the couch – although sometimes she would leave her daughter for a few moments to see to the children who had now gone without supervision for more than two days, and then the crowd huddling together in the room would respectfully part in order to let her through – and the only thing reflected now in the windows concealing the black Petersburg night was the Madonna and Child, floating in the clouds and deprived of their traditional holy guardians, because the approaching throng blocked the light from the candles burning on the desk, and their flames could no longer be reflected – and Dr Koshlakov would occasionally bend over the couch slightly to feel the dying man's already weak and uneven pulse, mostly, it seemed, for the sake of appearances, and when Dr Cherepnin arrived to join his colleague and, removing from his waistcoat pocket a silver watch and chain just as big as Koshlakov's, placed his hand on the dying man's wrist, it was already scarcely possible to feel any pulse at all.

A thin, scarcely perceptible thread still connected him with this world, but it, too, was growing weaker with every minute – the dying man was sinking inexorably into a deep, bottomless abyss resembling the hollow cone of a volcano, although it seemed to him that he was actually clambering up the highest mountain in the world, much higher than any other he had climbed or attempted to climb, and it seemed that he walked up a straight, light, crystal path, moving so easily that he did not appear to be going up at all, but descending, and at times he even thought that he was floating on invisible wings, and at the end of this path, on the very peak of the mountain, a bright sun shone, reflected in the crystal over which he was gliding and, when he reached the summit and the sun momentarily blinded him, he saw how low and insignificant those mountains were, where he had struggled upward before – nothing but tiny, wretched hills, and from the summit of this gigantic mountain was unveiled before him not only the earth with the vanity of its inhabitants, but the whole of the universe with its huge, bright stars, and for a moment there were revealed to him all the terrible secrets of those distant planets, but at that moment the sun was extinguished and he sank down into terrible, fathomless darkness.

The circle of onlookers had now almost closed completely, and a scarcely perceptible sigh of relief and a restrained whispering passed through the ranks of those present, as happens in the theatre when the culmination of the plot is succeeded by the dénouement – and his final heartbeat was recorded by Dr Cherepnin when he placed his stethoscope against the dying man's chest, the stethoscope which was later to be preserved as a family heirloom – and according to Anna Grigor'yevna this occurred at eight-thirty-eight in the evening – although the writer Markevich, who was one of the group of onlookers, in his newspaper account of those last hours, registered the moment of death as eight-thirty-six – and so the assembled company slowly dispersed with sorrowful faces befitting the occasion, although their expressions almost took on a kind of animation the nearer they got to the entrance-hall, as did their whispering which gradually rose into worldly conversation and even business discussion, and leading them all was, of course, Grigorovich, who, performing his intricate steps on the staircase, invited the dispersing visitors to follow his example.

After the departure of the guests, the lights were lit in all the rooms, as though there was some kind of a celebration in the house, and the doors were more or less all left open – and when it came to the moment of washing the body, Anna Grigor'yevna's brother arrived unexpectedly, having left Moscow that morning and knowing nothing of his brother-in-law's decease, and it was only the presence of a few common folk dressed in long cloth jackets stamping about on the staircase, talking about ordering a coffin for some dead writer that suggested to him the terrible thought, and a few moments later Anna Grigor'yevna was already weeping on her brother's shoulder – and while the body was being washed, Suvorin arrived straight from the theatre where he had been watching a play by Victor Hugo starring Mme Strepetova, and he was startled by the whiteness of the dead man's body and by the fact that this body, now no more than a shell, was being turned over and placed on straw which in penal servitude had no doubt served as bedding a hundred times for the former possessor of this body.

By midnight everything was ready – the deceased was lying on a table placed diagonally across the room, his features austere and tranquil as is always the case with dead people and as he was depicted by Kramskoy who arrived the next morning with paints and easel, and beneath the icon above his head a lamp had been lit and candles had been placed in his hands crossed on his chest, and until four or five in the morning, lights were burning in every room – and now, as I looked, all the windows in the building opposite where I was standing were dark, as if nobody lived there any more, and only in the windows at the corner point of the house, symbolizing, as did all the corners of buildings where he chose to live, that peak which he strove eternally to reach, only in these windows were there vague flickers and glimmers of light – probably the distant reflections of the nocturnal carnival of light on Nevsky, and just as dark were the enormous plate-glass windows of the Vladimir Church, now turned into some warehouse or depot.

The wind at the crossroads was blowing from all four sides, raising the snow and forming a kind of blizzard – I went up close to the building – the sign placed at the corner read 'Dostoyevsky Street' but for some reason I preferred to think of it as 'Yamskaya Street', as it used to be known before it was renamed – and I walked past the building down Yamskaya marked by a sparse row of dim street-lights disappearing somewhere into the distance, past a series of other similar tenement buildings with four or five storeys and deep, black-arched entrances leading into fathomless wells of courtyards, typical of Petersburg – and I even walked into one of them so as to feel the atmosphere more intensely – and from this deserted courtyard, enclosed by the four inner walls of the building, you could pass through another pitch-black entrance-way into the next courtyard, just as black and quandrangular and again with its own archway leading into the next courtyard.

I walked down the almost deserted, snow-covered Yamskaya Street into piles of snow heaped up along the pavements and a blizzard playing in between them, and my boots, lit up by the snow, returned its light as though I were wearing white felt boots – walking on past thick-walled buildings with silent, dark or dimly glowing windows, as though the electricity was burning at half-power or there were oil-lamps being used, as during the war, and neatly nailed beside the entrance to one of these buildings was a sign saying: 'Close the door firmly, save heat!', and in my mind's eye I saw Leningrad during the blockade, as I pictured it to myself from newspapers, books and eyewitness accounts, especially Gilya's tales – and most probably this city lacks sufficient warmth to the present day, or else the memory of that terrible winter has remained ineradicable.

Yamskaya, without turning, changed into another street, just as straight and snow-covered with the same line of street-lights disappearing into the distance – what, in fact, was I doing here? – why was I so strangely attracted and enticed by the life of this man who despised me and my kind (and deliberately so or with his eyes wide open, as he liked to put it)? – why had I come here under cover of darkness, walking along these empty and godforsaken streets like a thief? – why, when visiting his museum near the Kuznechny Market or other places connected with him, had I kept somehow to the side or trailed behind, as if I had turned up there by accident and none of it really interested me? – and were not my recent visions at Gilya's, in which, at the end, he turned into Isaiah Fomich, only the pathetic attempt of my subconscious mind to 'legitimize' my passion?

The street which I followed, continuing to reflect its light on my boots, might take me too far out of my way, into a district which I did not know and from which it would be difficult to extricate myself – so I turned down one of the side-streets and soon caught sight of the life-saving Ligovka and its trams – Svechnoy Lane it was called, and a certain Borovaya Street ran off from it somewhere, both of them old names, unchanged from a hundred years ago, and I thought that he must have passed this way himself more than once – and where the two streets forked there was an old chapel or a decapitated church, surrounded by glistening white snow – and it was almost completely light here, whether from the proximity of the Ligovka or the gleaming snow, and a family – the parents, badly and poorly dressed, accompanied by their seven- or eight-year-old daughter, also wearing a very threadbare overcoat – was walking past this former chapel or church with their pale Finnish faces, the father trailing a little behind with staggering steps, then catching up with his wife and daughter before all three suddenly fell into a snow-drift with the girl jumping up first and, shaking the snow off herself, beginning to say something quickly and angrily to her parents who seemed quite unable to get to their feet, but when they finally managed it and proceeded on their way, I could see that the mother was staggering unsteadily too – and the girl went on ahead, like a guide, or perhaps she was simply ashamed of her parents – and in the haloes around the street-lights on Svechnoy Lane snowflakes were slowly circling – I was approaching the Ligovka, and somewhere behind me was a semi-dark, endlessly straight street all covered in snow which the wind was piling into drifts, lined with silent tenement buildings and with the darkest and most silent of all – at the corner.

A few minutes later I was already in the tram heading towards Gilya's house, and half an hour after that I was once again chatting with her, sitting on Mozya's sofa, as she told me about the Blockade, about Mozya, about the year '37, and outside lay the wintry Petersburg night, and each time a tram clattered past down below, the whole house together with Mozya's lamp shuddered, like a ship straining at its moorings.

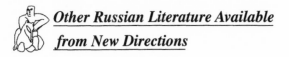

Other Russian Literature Available from New Directions

NINA BERBEROVA
The Billancourt Tales
The Book of Happiness
Cape of Storms
The Ladies from St. Petersburg
The Tattered Cloak

MIKHAIL BULGAKOV
Flight & Bliss
The Life of Monsieur de Molière

VLADIMIR NABOKOV
Laughter in the Dark
Nikolai Gogol
The Real Life of Sebastian Knight

BORIS PASTERNAK
Safe Conduct

VICTOR PELEVIN
The Blue Lantern & Other Stories
Four by Pelevin
Omon Ra
A Werewolf Problem in Central Russia
The Yellow Arrow

ZINOVY ZINIK
One-Way Ticket